buying dad

HARLYN AIZLEY

buying dad
ONE WOMAN'S SEARCH FOR THE PERFECT SPERM DONOR

alyson books
los angeles

MANUFACTURED IN THE UNITED STATES OF AMERICA.

THIS TRADE PAPERBACK ORIGINAL IS PUBLISHED BY ALYSON PUBLICATIONS,
P.O. BOX 4371, LOS ANGELES, CALIFORNIA 90078-4371.
DISTRIBUTION IN THE UNITED KINGDOM BY
TURNAROUND PUBLISHER SERVICES LTD.,
UNIT 3, OLYMPIA TRADING ESTATE, COBURG ROAD, WOOD GREEN,
LONDON N22 6TZ ENGLAND.

FIRST EDITION: JULY 2003

03 04 05 06 07 **a** 10 9 8 7 6 5 4 3 2 1

ISBN 1-55583-755-7

LIBRARY OF CONGRESS CATALOGING-IN-PUBLICATION DATA
  AIZLEY, HARLYN.
    BUYING DAD : ONE WOMAN'S SEARCH FOR THE PERFECT SPERM DONOR /
  HARLYN AIZLEY.—1ST ED.
      ISBN 1-55583-755-7 (PBK.)
      1. ARTIFICIAL INSEMINATION, HUMAN—SOCIAL ASPECTS. 2. LESBIAN
  COUPLES. I. TITLE.
  HQ761.A37 2003
  306.87—DC21   2003043793

CREDITS
COVER PHOTOGRAPHY BY JENNIFER CHEUNG.
COVER DESIGN BY MATT SAMS.

In loving memory of Sandra Fox Aizley
and
For Betsy

Either the well was very deep, or she fell very slowly, for she had plenty of time as she went down to look about her and to wonder what was going to happen next.

—Lewis Carroll,
Alice's Adventures in Wonderland

PART ONE

The Decision

I'm Not Forty

It's my thirty-eighth birthday, and I'm throwing myself a huge party. All day long people wander across the yard with their beers and burgers to ask me, "How does it feel to be forty?" I guess the party is so big they figure it for a milestone, some big fat divisible-by-ten occasion. My girlfriend, Faith, is at the grill. My mother and her friends line the back fence in assorted lawn chairs. There are three-year-olds and six-year-olds. There's my seventy-year-old cousin and her fifty-two year-old girlfriend. There are teachers and doctors and lawyers, a maniacal Cairn terrier, and a very docile Pekepoo.

At some point between the flipping of the last burger and the presentation of the cake, I climb to the top of the back stairs and shout at the top of my lungs, "I'm not forty!" It feels good. Really good. Because it's one thing being childless at thirty-eight, and totally another thing being childless at forty. Without telling anyone—including Faith—I have thrown myself a shit-or-get-off-the-pot party, an "Oh, my God, you're forty! Ha, ha, no you're not!" way of scaring myself into motherhood.

It was not so long ago that embarking on a life of same-sex love freed a woman from the ticking of her biological clock. Until just several years ago the only lesbians I knew with children were those who had been married very early on in their sexual careers. It even seemed at some point that as being gay became easier and more acceptable there was going to be a slow extinction of lesbian mothers because fewer women were going to get married in the first place. However, just as the gay nation inched ever onward in the media, the workplace, and our collective consciousness, so too did reproductive science follow suit.

Suddenly it's the twenty-first century and not only have sitcom characters and talk show hosts come roaring out of the closet, but those sticky bastions of anonymous masturbation once reserved for heterosexual couples struggling with male fertility are now ardent soldiers in the lesbian revolution. Lesbians are accessing sperm banks! And because a buck is a buck, sperm banks are marketing to lesbians! Sure, it's still possible to catch a cold shoulder or a decidedly unhelpful technician at one or another homophobic sperm bank across the nation. But with the wealth of others, those are easily avoidable. In fact, there are sperm banks all across the United States and abroad from which to choose. There are fertility clinics and private gynecologists in every city available to assist women and their partners in the process of insemination. Basically, a woman no longer needs a man to have a baby—at least she doesn't need to share her bed or bathroom with one.

For Jewish gay Gemini neurotics like myself this is mixed news. It means we have not been spared, after all, having to face the inevitable *tick tick tick* of our biological clocks. It means Faith and I will have to have countless long discussions about whether to have a baby. It means we may not rest easily in our vacancy-decontrolled one-bedroom apartment in Harvard Square, or on the fact that Faith can just make ends meet as a musician. It means we have to take responsibility for our lifestyle and our potentially childless future. It means we may have to grow up.

Maybe Only Freaks Have Two Mommies

(To Know or Not to Know)

Over dinner one evening, my three-year-old friend, Simone, looks lovingly at her father and informs me, "Daddies sound kind of like moose."

But what if there is no moose in the family? What if a little girl or boy is raised by two doe-a-deers? Do children need a moose, a tall, deep-voiced stubbly-chinned parent strong enough to lift them with one arm and toss them into the air? Someone to climb on top of and watch, mesmerized, as he mows the lawn, fixes the dishwasher, builds a cabinet, or replaces the engine of a car? Can being raised by two doe-a-deers possibly prepare a child for the coed world? Don't children, both male and female, need a man in order to develop their inner Yin? Or is it Yang?

Friends say that children relate to two separate adults as different and opposing beings regardless of their gender, that the whole mommy-and-a-moose thing is just one version of parenting. That there are, in fact, so many other options: two moose, mommy alone, mommy and grandma, mommy and a couple of aunts and uncles, or perhaps just one single-parent moose. Maybe my fear of not having a moose around to represent the other sex is a projection of my own homophobia, my own doubts as to the validity of Faith and me as parents.

"Do you like moose?" I ask Simone, hoping her wise three-year-old answer somehow will allay my fears.

"I like Arthur."

"Do you like Bambi?"

"Who's Bambi?"

"A deer. A female deer."

"What's female?"

We put our faith in the fact that it comes down to love, to adults providing a child with enough love and security from which he or she can bound into the world and learn all that is not available at home. After all, none of us are raised by "everyman." Some moose are rarely home, some know how to catch and throw a ball, while others cook and play guitar. And some doe-a-deers build fires and change tires.

To the argument that gay parents will create gay children, I have only this to say: Every homosexual I know, male or female, was raised by two heterosexuals.

Let the games begin.

While there are those women, gay and straight, who have known for as long as they can remember that one day they want to be a mother, others of us have spent most of our adult lives waiting to be swept away by even the shadow of a maternal urge. After college, I told myself not to worry; by thirty I definitely would have an interest in taking care of living creatures aside from plants and dogs. In my early thirties it was clear I was a late bloomer and likely would not host the mommy drive until age thirty-five. At thirty-five, still more interested in travel and sleeping in than getting my genes into the next generation, I allowed myself a couple more years of self-centered, responsibility-free narcissism. At thirty-eight, I threw myself the "you're forty" party, hoping to impregnate myself with maternal desire.

The thing that finally did it was entirely unexpected. My grandmother died. And my mother was diagnosed with cancer. All within the same six months. It was the loss of one source of unconditional love and the threatened loss of another that drove me to sit Faith down and start the first of hundreds of conversations about whether or not we wanted to have a family. It took us a year to decide, and then, of course, we had to find some sperm.

The first question we ask ourselves is the simple question any lesbian couple must ask themselves after deciding to have a family: Who's going first? For us the answer is easy; at least it's tangible. I'm thirty-eight, Faith thirty-five. Age before fertility. We decide I'll try to get pregnant first and then, after a year or two of diapers and sleepless nights, Faith will attempt the same. With the same donor. This brings us to the next question, which is not nearly as simple: Would we like to know the father of our child?

Faith answers yes. Me, a resounding no.

Faith and I are a lot like those little black-and-white dog magnets you can buy for a quarter at road-stop vending machines. We're brunette and dirty-blond versions of the same thing: a short Jewish lesbian in jeans and a T-shirt. Lip balm. Fleece. Haircuts twice a year. Highlights once every two years or whenever we visit our sisters in Los Angeles. But aside from the aesthetic and anatomic similarities, Faith and I are as different as, well, a double espresso and a cup of bancha tea. Working from the Her/Me paradigm, we fall into the following categories: Extrovert/Introvert. Patient/Impatient. MTV/PBS. Anal Expulsive/Anal Retentive. Known Donor/Unknown Donor.

In the year that we spend agonizing over it, the known versus unknown donor dilemma becomes a metaphor, sometimes figurative, sometimes literal, for all of the differences between us. It reminds us that we are two separate people, managing to live together only by the grace of God and sheer willpower. Thankfully, by the time the known/unknown donor question lands like a bomb in the middle of our relationship, we have already been together six years. Thankfully, in the year that we already spent deciding whether or not to have a family we managed to buy a house, thereby providing a legal hurdle to the dissolution of our relationship—because this decision could kill us, standing as it does like a monument to our two opposing wills.

The known versus unknown donor conversation takes place in hotel rooms when we are supposed to be on vacation, over the telephone, at the kitchen table, in front of our sisters. It ranges from a gentle sharing of opinion to shouts from one bicycle to another on a dirt path at Cape Cod to urgent tear-filled pleas in the middle of the night.

Faith, the people person, argues that it is in the best interest of our children to know their father. She wants to know what the father of our children looks like, what he sounds like, whether he has good taste in clothes. She worries that an anonymous donor will come looking for us, that he will lie about his medical history, that he will resemble every crazy and unappealing man who ever has undressed us with his greasy eyes. It is primal, Faith's aversion to an unknown donor. It is about preserving the sanctity of her genes, her heritage. She speaks for the species. Women have not evolved with two eyes for nothing. We see so that we may avoid mating with total dweebs.

I, on the other hand, am a freak obsessed with privacy. I guard my space with the ferocity of a pit bull. It takes all I have to creak open the door of my psyche and relinquish control enough to manage intimacy with one person. Imagine adding another to the equation! I worry that taking sperm from a man and having his child would instantly involve him as a permanent fixture in our life, someone with whom we must compromise, negotiate, or have over for dinner even when I need to be alone, even we need to be alone as a family. All of that, and he may not even be someone I love. At least I love Faith. At least this all began with the splendid privacy-defying urge to hold her in my arms.

We are at a stalemate. And so we decide to attend a workshop.

The workshop is sponsored by a local clinic specializing in all matters gay and lesbian. It is designed to address the issue of lesbian parenting and promises to spend at least a portion of the two-hour, sixty-five-dollar session talking about our problem: known versus unknown donors. Faith and I arrive separately from work, each with a little pad of paper and a pen.

There are at least fifteen other couples in the room, of all shapes and sizes. All women. All gay. All day. For a brief, terrible moment I think, *Lesbian parents?!* I look over at Faith. She is white as a ghost.

Differences aside, part of what bonds Faith and me is the myth we share that, despite our intimate relationship, we are not lesbians. Sure, we have sex with women and can count on one hand the number of times in the last three years either of us has worn a dress. Still, neither of us is a man-hating flannel-loving she-man. I can't even hit a ball. Both of us were brought up in stable, albeit unsatisfying, upper-middle-class Jewish households. Our families loved us dearly, sent us to college. They sighed, kvetched, but ultimately embraced us after we came out. We never needed to find new family in an identity, never needed to create a world of acceptance, because our world always accepted us. So sitting in the midst of the lesbian nation is unnerving. We want our sisters. We want our mothers. We want to figure out the answer to our big insurmountable problem and go home.

The workshop leaders inform us that while all sperm banks require donors to sign waivers relinquishing their rights to whatever offspring are conceived from their sperm, only one state in the country reinforces that waiver (i.e., would throw out of court any donor's attempt to gain access to birth records). And that state, of course, is the one at the end of the rainbow, California. We learn that some donors agree to allow their offspring to locate them when they are eighteen years old. We learn that many men are rejected as potential sperm donors, so those whose semen as well as personalities pass the test are the cream of the crop, so to speak.

Faith scribbles down notes about frozen semen and motility counts. I jot down the legal issues that need to be addressed in any contract with a known donor. At the end of the workshop, women gather round to read sample donor profiles (the full medical history and personal essay written by a donor). There is a table of tea and soft drinks, cookies and crackers. We pick up brochures, offer tight smiles to the other couples, and are just about to release the tense breaths we inhaled over an hour ago when a woman runs into the conference room crying, "All of our cars have been broken into!"

That's it, I think. No more lesbian group hugs. No more changing the world.

But try telling that to my lesbian local musical celebrity girlfriend, who has more difficulty remembering to turn off the porch light than she does being an out gay girl in public.

"How about that?" I say, trying not to sound too internally homophobic.

It turns out that all but a few of the cars parked in the clinic's parking lot sport broken windows. Ironically, only Faith's car and two others have been spared, but there is a gaping hole where my driver's side window used to be and bits of blue glass scattered like crushed ice all over the seat and floor. There is an air of gay bashing to the whole event. This is why I am afraid to identify as a lesbian, I think. Maybe it's not fair to bring children into this world to be raised by an oppressed minority.

Faith doesn't buy the gay-bashing theory. She thinks it's just bad city luck. She reassures me oppressed minorities have been raising families since the beginning of time and that of all reasons should not be the one that deters us from having children. Her optimism reminds me how nice it is to be with someone who, unlike myself, is not introverted and paranoid, someone who gives other people the benefit of the doubt and opens my world to adventure I might otherwise miss. I lay down my distrust and allow myself to consider how nice it really would be to know the father of our children. I imagine the right man in the most ideal circumstances and how we might enlarge our dwindling families. I imagine my mother and his at Thanksgiving or Hanukkah. I imagine him taking on an uncle-ish role, sending birthday presents and providing the children with a weekend getaway every now and again. There is relief in knowing and possibly loving the source of the genetic material that will bind with my own.

"All right, but we have to agree on who it is," I tell Faith as we brush broken glass from the driver's seat of my car.

"Absolutely."

So, at thirty-eight and counting, we begin looking for a sperm daddy.

In all honesty, this is not exactly the first time we have mulled over potential known donors. In much the same way one pores over baby names at the first thought of pregnancy, so have we at one time or another considered the possibility of getting sperm from every one of our closest male friends. If you count all the times we've said, "Hey, you want to donate sperm?" to men at parties, we likely have asked between ten and twenty men to father our children. If you add all the times Faith has thrown the question out to her audience at a gig, that number increases to something like 4,000 or 5,000. But in the final roundup there are only two serious potential candidates.

$\mathcal{KD}$1

Known Donor Number One (KD1) is a strapping heterosexual who actually approaches us about donating sperm. We're watching the Red Sox getting creamed one night when KD1 announces there's something he's been wanting to tell us. KD1 is the drummer in Faith's band. We brace ourselves for the news that he's leaving the group. I start thinking of all the other possible drummers that will come into our life now, big bonehead guys with no respect for Faith's and my relationship, or maybe some stud who will sweep Faith off her gay feet. And then I get jealous because other people always have the courage to pack up and move and for years I was afraid to leave Boston for fear of destroying my mother. And then, after 9,000 years of therapy, I finally was able to imagine separating, but my mother was diagnosed with cancer and of course I'm not going anywhere. Faith is looking nervous, and I know at least the part about finding a new drummer is swimming around in her head as well. KD1 shuffles from one foot to the other. He says he's been thinking really hard about us becoming parents and how much he would like to help make that happen, and though he isn't a hundred percent certain he'll do it, he'd like to throw out the idea of being our sperm donor.

Wow.

We are so relieved that he isn't leaving or making some other terrible announcement that we both start to cry. And then KD1 cries, because he thinks we are so moved by what he is saying, which we are, but there also is that huge element of relief.

KD1 is the first man who has approached us about donating sperm who is not obese, lecherous, or mentally unstable. Over the years offering up one's love juice seems to have become a way for men to express their attraction to lesbians otherwise unavailable. It's as if they're saying, *Hey, if I can't screw you, the least you could do is let me knock you up.* But KD1 is handsome and healthy and good-hearted. He even has a girlfriend who supports him in this decision. It's all so amazing and unexpected that part of me wants him to whip it out right now. Instead, after the initial surprise has worn off, we laugh and wipe our eyes and decide to meet monthly for six months to talk it over. And then, of course, everything changes.

Our monthly meetings consist of Faith and me making dinner for KD1 and then listening for three hours as he shares with us all of his thoughts and feelings about sperm donation and parenthood. We hear about what it means to his therapist, his girlfriend, his seven Irish Catholic siblings (one sister—a lesbian—bawls to him nightly over the phone, "Don't do it! You're ruining your life!"), and his future children. He assures us that even though no one in his family likes the idea, he is fairly certain they will be nice to the baby.

Faith is thrilled. She has a Polaroid of KD1 she props up on our dresser. Each night she picks it up and selects another feature of KD1's to meld in her mind with mine.

"Your baby will have the bluest eyes," she says. Such strong cheekbones, great skin.

After one such dinner, while Faith is in the kitchen cleaning and KD1 and I are alone in the dining room, he mentions money. As in, "You know, I might feel differently if you guys didn't have any money, but you have a great house and seem to be doing well." Alarms go off in my head. But I am a recluse, an introvert. I thought I was being gay-bashed when someone was probably just looking for a warm blanket or fifty cents. So I try to muffle the alarms, to push them out the back door of my untrusting mind and smile.

KD1 continues, "And the house looks safe. You'll probably have to childproof your outlets, but there's time for that."

Ding! Ding! Ding!

Faith brings dessert in to us. She is so happy and unsuspecting. I want to comfort her, put a hand on her shoulder, and support her as she receives the blow. I wait for KD1 to mention our financial status and child-safety issues to Faith, but he doesn't.

"I love sherbet," he says as Faith hands him a bowl.

After he leaves, she is more thrilled than ever.

A month later I'm visiting my sister, Carrie, in Los Angeles, taking a precious sun-filled stroll along the beach in February. I'm telling her about KD1, about how nice it is to be able to picture the father of our children even if his family already hates me and Faith. I tell her about shared birthdays and holidays and how his hostile sisters will come over and be nice to our baby but not to us and maybe one day even sue us for custody. I tell her how Faith and I used to discuss what it will be like to be parents, and how we now discuss what it will be like for KD1 to be a parent. I tell her how nice it is to be thirty-eight years old and have someone come into my home and comment on my financial situation and the status of my electrical outlets. I'm walking so fast she has to trot to keep up with me. I'm trying to sound all communal and happy, glowing even in anticipation, despite my furrowed brow, but my sister knows me too well.

"Sounds like hell," she says.

Five minutes later I'm at a Venice Beach pay phone crying to Faith, "I can't do it. This has become all about him and we're not even raising his child yet. Imagine how he and his mean-ass family will feel if we have a son who looks like him. It's like bringing a child into divorce rather than love. And I didn't even tell you about the outlets."

I'm ready for a fight, for a debate, for a battle of the moms. But thankfully, Faith agrees. She's been feeling the same.

Goodbye, KD1. Though we have not let go of the known donor fantasy, we tell him we are looking into anonymous donors. KD1 is so respectful of our decision that the night after we break the news we lie in bed wondering whether we have made the right choice. The following week he comes over and helps us set up our computer so that we can begin browsing sperm bank Web sites. In return we make him dinner and listen for two hours as he goes on about his current girlfriend.

KD2

Faith and I decide that at least part of the problem with KD1 was proximity. What we need is a known donor who doesn't come over twice a week to rehearse with the band. We need someone who lives out of town. Someone whose presence is infrequent enough as to lend him that uncle-ish air. Someone whose family likes the idea of his donating sperm. Someone familiar. Someone Jewish. Someone gay.

Enter KD2. KD2 is a childhood friend of Faith's. He is gay, Jewish, and lives in Chicago. Faith remembers posing the question of whether he would ever consider donating sperm, hypothetically, a year or so ago, and she calls him now to see if he remembers.

KD2 remembers. Apparently, he has been thinking about it ever since. He even entered therapy to discuss it further. He told his mother and his father, both of whom were thrilled. He was only waiting for us to bring it up again, so as not to apply any undue pressure. It is frightening but exciting, the thought of providing a child with an extra set of Jewish grandparents, doting aunts and uncles, maybe a little something for the college fund. You can't have too much love around.

We begin biweekly phone meetings with KD2. The meetings address the role he will play in the child's life. We hope for uncle. He suggests long-distance dad. We compromise on grandfather. We discuss financial obligations—none as far as we are concerned—and the right for Faith and me to reserve all parental rights. At the end of our first conversation, KD2 asks, "What do you think of the name 'Tyler' for a boy?"

During our next conversation we gently ask KD2 if he really is comfortable having no say over such child-rearing issues as schooling, circumcision—oh, and naming the child—to cite a few.

He pauses. "Well," he finally says, "I guess I just hope I'd be someone you'd want to talk with about such things, you know, as a friend, for another opinion."

By the way, he adds later in the conversation, will his name appear on the birth certificate? He realizes he may not have a say over the child's name, but he would like to go on record as the biological father.

Inside my head, alarms are going off all over the place. But his parents are thrilled, his brother and sister all love the idea. He lives two hours away by plane—how involved could he be, after all? Faith is more enthusiastic than ever about us becoming parents. I convince myself all will be well. What's a birth certificate between friends? We mail him a sample legal agreement and arrange to see him in person to finalize the negotiations next month when we are in Chicago visiting Faith's family.

It's a sunny Chicago afternoon in May when we meet KD2 for lunch at an outdoor café. KD2 has read the legal contract and agrees to all aspects of it. He is so excited to give us sperm. He tells us how much he loves children and how he has been telling all of his friends about becoming a father. He corrects himself with a smile, "I mean a grandfather."

I will turn thirty-nine next month and time feels so short and I want so much to please Faith and become communal and enable our children to know their father. "Okay," I say. "Let's start next month."

Faith doesn't respond. She doesn't say, "Great!" Or, "I'm so excited!" Or, "I can't wait!" She just orders herself a cup of coffee.

KD2 tells us he was planning to take a week off from work in June, so why don't we arrange it so that the week coincides with my intended ovulation? He's always wanted to see Boston. Even though he really only needs to come (joke) for three or four days, why doesn't he stay for a week?

I am communal and open and social, so I say, "Sure," and excuse myself to go to our car, which is parked across the street, so that I can get my date book and arrange for KD2 to visit the next time I'm ovulating. I assume Faith will have rejoined the conversation by the time I return, that she will have pulled out her date book or taken KD2's hand or something equally positive and affirming. After all, in a way I am doing this for her. Or us. For our unborn child, who will be light-years healthier for having been raised by mommies who enabled him or her to know their biological father, despite the insanity that relationship will cause one of said mommies. I mean, which is better, knowing your dad or having a happy mom? This is the first sacrifice of parenthood. Right?

Green light. I race across the street, grab my date book from my bag in the back of Faith's mother's Civic, slam the door closed, and am about to head back to the café when I'm stopped in my tracks by a red light. The light remains red just long enough for me to stand on the corner and look over at them, the woman I have made a lifetime commitment to and a man I really hardly know and have no interest in marrying, so to speak. What is he doing in this picture? I have to admit now that I am all the way across the street, with some distance on the matter so that I am just so *not* communal, and when KD2 offered to visit for a week my first thought was, *A whole week?!* If I'm hesitant about spending a week with him, how will I handle a lifetime? And doesn't he talk a lot? And how about his eyes? They're squinty, like my father's. The combination of his genes and mine will make little squints, children all cheeks and no eyes. And just imagine sending our son or daughter to visit for a week when KD2 has a houseful of gay men complaining about our kid's dirty fingernails. And what if he gets involved with someone who hates women or hates children? And come on now, isn't having a happy mentally healthy mommy *way* more important than knowing your freaking dad? And why hasn't Faith said a word in the past fifteen minutes?

Faith drives us back to her mother's house and neither of us speaks for what feels like six hours. Finally I eke out, "So?"

Faith replies, "Well, that happened pretty fast."

Pretty fast? It's the end of May and we've been interviewing possible donors since October. KD2 has been on the table for three months, not counting the year prior to that when he was thinking about it. I remind Faith that I'm turning thirty-nine in a few weeks and that we really need to start; I can't wait anymore. I won't wait. I agreed to a known donor and here he is, even if he has squinty eyes and talks too much.

"Maybe it's him," she says. "Maybe he's not the right man."

We review our profile of the "right man." Someone who knows our children but allows us total control over all aspects of child-rearing. Someone like an uncle, who will dote on our children without intruding upon our rein of power. Someone who visits only when invited and whose family does not put demands on holidays already stretched thin by our own families' divorces and diffusion across the United States.

Okay. So, basically, we want a handsome, smart, kind man to donate sperm to us and then blow like the wind out of our lives.

We both agree: It's impossible. And even if there were a man out there possessing the perfect combination of sensitivity and psychopathy, neither of us has the energy to go through another three months of negotiations. We dread telling KD2 the news. We don't have it in us to go through this again or to do this to another man.

Two weeks later, in an uncomfortable phone conversation, KD2 takes the news exactly as predicted. He is devastated, sad, angry. While KD2's reaction makes us feel horrible—as if we have deprived a gay man of his only chance to bring a child into this world—it also confirms that we've made the right decision. If he's this disappointed now, imagine how he might have felt after seeing his son or daughter being raised without him. If anything, KD2's response helps us take the next step.

Just a few weeks before my thirty-ninth birthday, we agree to make a family with anonymous sperm. I tell Faith I want to start by July. That gives us a month and a half to choose.

More often than ever, I find myself wishing I were with a man. On those days I assume that if I had chosen a man as my life partner instead of a woman, everything would be so much easier. I would have all the sperm I wanted as well as the blessing of society. I would be able to hold my partner's hand in public and have a house stocked with china and linen and all of the Pottery Barn kitchen supplies I would have gotten at my wedding. There would be someone to kill bugs and take out the garbage even if I did get home first from work. The doorknob on the front door would be fixed, and there would be more money in my IRA. A married friend tells me, "You have got to be kidding. It's like saying your life would be perfect if you were rich."

Well, that too.

Shop Shop Shop Till You Drop!

(THE SQUIRREL, THE JEW, AND THE NAVAJO)

There seem to be tons of sperm banks in the world to choose from. There are sperm banks in the friendly state of California. There are sperm banks in Georgia and Minnesota, Amsterdam and Virginia. There are sperm banks here in Boston, sperm banks specializing in the high-IQ sperm of medical students and law students, sperm banks stocked by struggling music students, and sperm banks stocked by married men with children just looking for a little extra money for the holidays. Because we are not married wives looking to find the perfect combination of facial features with which to duplicate an infertile husband, the genetic world is our oyster, and buying sperm is much like shopping at Sam's Club or Costco. There are so many choices, such mass quantities of hair, skin tone, and childhood diseases, of grandparents' hobbies and maternal aunts' educational backgrounds. And though none of it really matters—any parent will tell you, you get what you get—it certainly seems to as we cruise down the aisles with our genetic shopping list. Hmm, tall genes would be nice. Oh, look honey, math, and engineering skills!

You would think the weeding-out process could easily begin with race. I mean, why would we thrust on an innocent child not only an autographed copy of *Heather Has Two Mommies* but also the minefield of being biracial in our often less than open-minded world?

But Faith, still reeling from having stepped down from her known-donor platform, thinks we should purchase the sperm of a man of color. The roots of her reasoning are part nature and part nurture. On the nature side, Faith has been reading about genetic diseases in *The New York Times* and has learned all about Jewish cancer and Tay-Sachs and the fact that we are a small, inbred tribe filled with terrible recessive genes. Not to mention that her mother's golden retriever recently developed arthritis and my father's Newfoundland dysplasia, both ominous signs regarding Jews mating with Jews as far as Faith is concerned. She wants us to breed mixed-race children with strong constitutions and great hair.

On the nurture side, as a child growing up in the 1960s in Chicago's South Common neighborhood, Faith was one of only a handful of white children attending a primarily African-American school. "I've always wanted to be black," Faith says, without even a hint of white guilt.

You'd think it would be similar to dating, choosing a mate, this ability to carefully select the sperm source of our child. But if the acquisition of an object of affection is the result of an unpredictable and spontaneous explosion of the heart, then the acquisition of anonymous sperm is exactly the opposite. It is calculated and particular. It's like selective breeding. And as such, it can bring to light all of our most rank and stinky inner racism and classism, SAT-ism and sizeism, even homophobia. While I have no doubt as to the health and sanity of mixed-race children, the idea of adding that chip to the gay mommies chip just freaks me out. Besides, I feel we would owe a mixed-race child a particular cultural experience that I'm not sure we can provide.

"What would you tell the children?" I ask Faith. "When they come home from school and say they are sick and tired of being tormented because their mothers are gay, and by the way, were you just being sadistic when you added race to the pot?"

"Well, how about a man who's a quarter Navajo?"

And then there's me. From age seven to twelve I wanted to be Native American. I turned my bedroom into a makeshift teepee, learned how to use a bow and arrow, and wore a little Native American costume complete with feather headdress and red tights all around my northern New Jersey neighborhood. So, for all of the wrong reasons, "A quarter Navajo I can live with," I tell Faith. And she willingly lets go her dream of our child becoming the next Sarah Vaughan or Langston Hughes.

We have donor catalogs from five different sperm banks strewn across the living room floor. We've downloaded another five on the computer. By ruling out all non-Anglos except the quarter Navajo, we have narrowed the field by about three percent.

Our next step in weeding out donors is to look for only "yes donors." We have decided that if our children cannot know their father while growing up, at least they can have the option of knowing him at some point later in their life. Yes donors agree to allow the sperm bank to arrange a one-time meeting between them and each of their offspring should the child request such a meeting after his or her eighteenth birthday. There are far fewer yes donors than no donors, and for now we're grateful, as that narrows the field dramatically. They're also more expensive (we learn later that yes donors are paid more for their "donations"), costing an extra twenty-five dollars per vial. We deem it a small price to pay for the option and our child's well-being, far less expensive than counseling or any kind of behavioral therapy.

It's early June, and even though there isn't much time left before our self-imposed deadline, getting Faith to sit down with me and go over donor catalogs is a lot like trying to brush the cat. The cat kind of loves it and hates it all at the same time, so he leads me around the house, pausing only for brief moments here and there to allow me a few strokes and then taking off again with a start, as if it just dawned on him what it is that I'm doing and, wait a minute, what the hell is going on here?!

Faith is good for about three minutes at a time, and then she gets fidgety and restless and mumbles things like, "I just wish I could see what they look like," before squirming away. Though any therapist would insist this be a joint project, I ask Faith if she'd like me to do the initial scan— i.e., read through the catalogs to sort by height, hair color, eye color, educational background, religion—and thereby spare her the tedious process of finding the final ten from which to choose. Then she'd only have to join me when we went to the clinic to look at the "long forms."

I know it all has to do with her ambivalence and that we may live to regret not putting the process on hold for a month to sort through her fear, but the *tick tick tick* is deafening now and I'm General Patton, leading us ever onward. I figure we'll have plenty of time to ambivalate when I'm six months pregnant.

Faith says no, she can do it. We make a date for a night this week to sit with the catalogs and select several finalists whose "long forms" we want to see.

Long forms are the whole story, containing the complete medical history of the donor as well as the medical history of his immediate and extended family. Some sperm banks include the donors' answers to a list of questions like "What is your favorite sport?" and "Do you like animals?" Most sperm banks also include a section where the donor can write a paragraph or two about why he has chosen to donate sperm in the first place. Long forms cost anywhere from twenty to thirty-five dollars each, so you want to either narrow down your final choices to a select few or have access to a clinic that stores long forms in a donor library.

Well, our date is going to be extra special because Faith found a sperm bank in Georgia that offers pictures of their donors! She is so excited. I haven't seen her this enthused since the days she fondled KD1's Polaroid. We call up the Georgia bank and they tell us that for a registration fee of one hundred dollars we can look online for the next six months at pictures of all of their donors. Fine. A hundred dollars. Fine. We read them our credit card number and postpone our date until it is processed.

I worry, but know better than to confess it to Faith, that Southern sperm donors are racist, anti-Semitic, homophobic, and pro-military. The night after we register with the Southern picture bank I dream I'm looking at photographs of the donors and they all look like characters from

Deliverance. There are blond men—and women(!)—with bad teeth and bulging pink lips.

I become obsessed with California sperm. I decide that in California struggling artists donate sperm, while in the South white supremacists bent on creating an Aryan nation donate in order to enhance their genetic load.

Our registration is complete, and tonight Faith and I have a date to view the pictures of the Southern bigots.

My father calls to see how "things are going." Whenever I talk to my father, despite my job and Faith's job and our semisolid savings, I refer to our plans for insemination as "our wedding"—as in, you just paid for Carrie's wedding, so think of this as "our wedding" and show equal ($) support. I feel disgusting about this, like a greedy, needy child, but I do it anyway. I can't help it. I'm certain it has to do with all sorts of past childhood issues of symmetry and fairness and sexuality, things that could better be worked out in therapy, but still I try. It's just that I'm so worried about where we'll get the money to raise a child. At night my mind races with fear and is host to all sorts of terrifying scenarios of destitution and impoverishment. I tell myself that most of the world raises happy children with far fewer resources than we have, that we're adults, privileged in so many ways, that we've been planning and preparing and will manage. While it's an enormous struggle to believe my own reassurances, still I chase Faith around with the brush and lead us ever onward. *Tick. Tick. Tick.*

The pictures are overwhelming. It's great to see them, and terrible and confusing to see them. They are our knights in shining armor; they are the good, wise men; they are freaks. What man in his right mind would donate sperm to strangers? Fortunately only two or three look really odd. Some are handsome. Most are average.

Believe it or not, we come to feel we shouldn't see them. That it's better to picture a donor in your mind, better to fantasize a man who looks like your partner, than to raise your family in the shadow of a stranger whose photo lurks upstairs in a locked file cabinet year after curious year like some sort of ghost daddy.

We wonder what it would be like for our children to know that we have a picture of their anonymous father. I can imagine not wanting to tell a child until he or she is old enough to look at the picture with some kind of understanding of the emotional enormity seeing it will entail. And then carrying the child of an unknown man whom you can picture and look for on the streets of New York or Boston or San Francisco is strangely horrifying. I know I would search for him everywhere, at work, in supermarkets, on the evening news.

Still, Faith and I scan the entire sperm bank, gawking at the faces. We are obsessed. And sure enough, despite our revulsion, we become interested in a few. One man we come to call "the Squirrel" (because he is five foot six and looks, well, like a squirrel, albeit a handsome Jewish one) appeals to us because in lieu of an essay as to why he has chosen to donate sperm, he has written a two-page letter to his unborn children. I think the Squirrel is someone we could manage having in our lives should our tiny squirrel children ever seek him out. He is mature and sophisticated, interested in classical music and literature. We can hold the precious letter for our children for years to come, present it to them in Tuscany or a cabin on the Russian River one summer on a family vacation. We think the Squirrel won't mind hearing that he impregnated lesbians. That is important. Some of the donors, those claiming allegiance to the Church of God, those who begin their essays with, "I'm a God-fearing man," are disasters waiting to happen eighteen years from now when Susie or Billy calls up and informs them, "My mommies just showed me your donor profile."

And then there's a man who looks like Matt Dillon. Faith is in love. Even though the Matt Dillon donor has a horrible genetic illness that runs through both sides of his family, Faith doesn't care. She confesses that all she wants is good-looking kids. That's why she wanted a known donor. That's why she wanted mixed-race children. That's why she wanted to at least see a picture. She goes on to reveal that the only reason she wanted to be involved with me when we first met was because I was attractive.

"It's all about looks," she murmurs. "I don't want ugly kids."

I should say something to the effect of, "Give me a break—you're just scared." Or, "You'll love your children no matter what they look like." But instead I say, "I'm not *that* good-looking."

"Yes, you are."

Though I'm secretly thrilled, I nix the genetic-disease guy—no room for negotiation—and we're back to work. We spend the next two hours looking at pictures of every donor under six feet three inches tall and weighing less than two hundred pounds.

One nice Jewish guy just plain old gives us the creeps. We're concerned about the Squirrel's height. Another Jew has cancer sprinkled throughout his family like kosher salt on a hard-boiled egg. We need more options.

And then we have it! With the help of the Picture Bank, we will conduct an experiment. We decide to read the essays of all of the ugliest, strangest-looking men and see if there's a correlation between strange appearance and strange writing. If so, we reason, we can more easily trust those donors without pictures who offer literate, competent, and kind enough sounding profiles.

We are geniuses. We are Nobel laureates. We are going to be good mothers.

It turns out that the absolutely most bizarre-looking men do indeed have the sparsest, oddest, most poorly written essays. We take our experiment one step further. We hypothesize next that we will feel most comfortable with a Jewish donor, indeed that Jewish donors will be the most attractive to us. It's a tribe thing. We figure because we are Jews ourselves, even the ickiest of our tribe will look warm and fuzzy and familiar. We'd rather go wrong with one of our own.

We look at all the Jews. Despite their varying medical histories, they're all good-looking enough, and all have gone to college. We redefine our search. We are looking for a Jew, with or without a picture, who has a decent medical history and a well-written essay. We rule out the creepy-looking Jew who I am convinced, from the look in his eye and the fact that at age thirty he moved home to work for his father, suffers from some form of mental illness. We rule out a very young bicycle-riding Jew because of the following statement: "I look forward to traveling to Paris one day to visit the Van Gough [sic] Museum." We rule out fat men, men with histories of acne, men whose distant uncles committed suicide. We rule out any man whose medical history reads like the *Principles of Internal Medicine*. We rule out one man because he sounds too good to be true and therefore probably is.

Out of the hundreds of possible anonymous sperm donors across the nation we are left with four: the Squirrel, Unibrow (a man who over and over again makes reference to his heavy dark eyebrows, as if out of moral obligation), Big Jew (six foot one), and Giant Jew (six foot three). There is only one thing left to do.

I make four little strips of paper and write the name of a donor on each and then fold them into tight squares.

I tell Faith, "Whichever you touch first is it."

She dips a tremulous hand into our future, pulls out a square, and slowly releases each of its nervous little folds.

"Squirrel," she says in a whisper.

"All right," I say, "two out of three."

In a last-ditch effort to broaden the field, we download the donor catalog of a small sperm bank in California and there find two perfect specimens. Both Jewish. Both referred to as "attractive" by whomever interviewed them and wrote their short entry in the catalog. Each is a yes donor. Good medical histories. Believable and kind essays as to why they have decided to donate. One is six feet tall, the other five foot ten and balding. We call California the next day. The six-footer is sold out. "Jewish donors sell out fast," the woman at the sperm bank tells us. So, desperately clinging to the myth that male pattern baldness is passed down by mothers, not fathers, we purchase all of Baldie's remaining vials.

I feel sick. I want to apologize to our unborn children for any mistake I may have made. For denying them thick, wavy, curly hair and physical beauty, all of which I suddenly fear they will never know.

And then suddenly I love him or her, this beautiful as-yet-unfertilized child who will have hair after all because male pattern baldness really is passed down along a mother's side of the family...isn't it? So our child/son will be doomed thanks to my father's hair pattern and not to my own lack of judgment. It's not my fault. I made the best decision I could.

We can't begin until next month as the sperm is still in quarantine, i.e., must pass one more HIV test. My days are numbered. I drink coffee, have white wine with dinner.

I am sad for the small Squirrel with the beautiful letter, nostalgic for the Unibrow. Sad for the rejected babies, some too short, some too dark, some just too elusive. Sad for the math and engineering skills, the athletic skills (Baldie is a writer and theater person like us, and therefore, I presume, gay), for not choosing to spread the genes of men whose families were lost in the Holocaust.

The sperm bank requires that I be tested for syphilis, gonorrhea, chlamydia, and HIV before they will send us sperm. Liability. It's all about liability. It's always something.

Always another hurdle. I start to develop symptoms. I have strange burning sensations in my nether regions. I tell Faith I think I have gonorrhea. She walks out of the room and turns on the television.

Girlfriends Who Spill

(THAT DIRTY VAG O' MINE
AND THE FERTILITY FASCISTS)

The first two specimens of the six we've reserved are ICI (intracervical)—semen that can be inserted into my vagina by anyone wielding an applicator. ICI semen is the real thing, unpasteurized, straight from the farm. The other four specimens are IUI (intrauterine)—semen that is prepped (i.e. "washed," so that it chemically resembles semen that already has passed through a woman's vagina) to be directly inserted into the uterus by a doctor or a nurse. IUI semen is more expensive, thanks to the careful bathing and cleansing it's undergone. Not to mention that having an IUI sample injected (via a catheter thread through the cervix) costs two hundred fifty dollars and hardly promises an atmosphere of romance and tranquility. Faith and I have decided that our first foray into conception should take place in the privacy of our own home. Why not see if we can get pregnant the romantic way, with a syringe and a glass of wine? If this fails, we'll have a three-way with a doctor at the fertility clinic.

Unfortunately, this means that Faith, a notorious spiller, will handle the one-hundred-sixty-five-dollar vials of ICI semen. Faith, though I love her dearly, holds all implements (pens, forks, spoons) too far from the base for maximum control. She holds them near the top, so that soup or corn or whatever it is she's trying to steer into her oral cavity dribbles off onto the table. I eye her daily, watching as she drops crumbs onto the floor, the sofa, watching the trail of chips, socks, papers that slip from her grip as she floats from room to room.

Faith? Faith is going to inseminate me? She will hold the syringe too far from the tip! She will spill one hundred and ninety dollars worth of semen onto my thigh! She will laugh and then I will get mad and then she will get mad and slam the vial down onto a pile of cat fur and lint! I have no trust whatsoever. I want to do it myself. And if I can't trust my own partner with a vial of semen, how can I trust her with a child? I do, though. I inherently trust her with a child, with an infant. I just don't trust her with a vial of semen, a bowl of ice cream, a bag of chips, a felt-tip marker.

In three days I will have my sex tests and also have my finger X-rayed. For three weeks the third finger of my left hand has been swollen and black-and-blue. I slammed it against the steel dressing room door at Canal Jeans in a fit of modesty on a trip to New York at the end of June. The nurse where I am teaching this summer told me to put my finger in a splint, so I went to the drugstore and bought one of those steel-on-one-side-blue-foam-on-the-other deals and have been wearing it ever since, and my finger has gone from bad to worse. But for three weeks I just could not be bothered. There is so much going on of more importance...or so I think.

I'm sure it has been said before, but I can't stop looking around the house at all of our pointy edges, poisonous plants, and overloaded outlets. There is the flaking plaster wall inside the bedroom closet, the extension cords that run across rooms like circus pranks to trip unsuspecting guests, or toddlers who have recently learned to walk. And then there is Shit Beach, an expanse of grit and dust at the far corner of bathroom, where the litter box resides. No matter how much we sweep and scoop, kitty litter and hardened balls of cat shit lie like jewels upon the floor. So, especially troubling is the rumor that cat shit is to pregnant women what kryptonite is to Superman, that touching it or perhaps even inhaling it can damage you and your fetus forever. I am doomed. Our one kitty poops so much we actually have two litter boxes, one in the basement and one in the bathroom, both of which have been my responsibility for the last seven and a half years because, after all, he is my cat. I remind Faith of my upcoming nine-month sabbatical from cat-poop duty.

She grimaces.

Like it matters. We each are all the time stepping on scattered hardened balls of poop with our bare feet. They get stuck to our kitty's long fur and then delicately drop off at odd times and, therefore, can be found in the living room, the kitchen, on top of the piano. Really, so what can we do?

And then there's lead...

We are afraid we will have gay children, that our gay genes plus the father's obviously gay genes (he is involved in theater and loves to cook and travel; besides, what other nice Jewish boy would sell his love juice but a gay one, interested, perhaps, in getting his genes into the next generation sans commitment) will create a tribe of queens and bull dykes.

"I hope our kids aren't gay," I confess in a homophobic whisper.

"Me too," Faith says. We are freaks.

It's just that lately I feel sick of homosexuality and its competitive chic, the way we have joined the monotony of mainstream culture rather than created a new world order.

I am sick of the gay gentrification that has whitewashed places like Provincetown. Sick of bulging abs and biceps. Sick of androgyny, fashion cuts, dark-rimmed glasses, and plain-front khakis.

I am at the doctor waiting for my syphilis/gonorrhea/chlamydia/HIV whore check. My finger, along for the ride, is black-and-blue and more conical at the middle joint than ever before. I vow to get pregnant even if they put me in a cast. Though what I really am thinking is that I hope my finger is not symptomatic of some horrible disease system I am too nervous to name. And! I have looked back at my physical exam reports from the last three years and noticed I have consistently low platelets, something apparently attributable to my blood not liking a particular test tube, but what if...? My heart races and I go pale. I am here to have a baby, but what if fate has something else in store for me, involving doctors and blood and my future as a parent? What if I am destined to coparent my girlfriend's children? Why is that bad? And if that is how I feel, how must Faith be feeling these days?

There is Bruce Springsteen playing in the waiting room. Shouldn't they be playing classical music or have no music playing at all?

We also worry about keloids and money, not necessarily in that order. We worry about keloids because a friend introduced us to his, a grotesque blob protruding from his left leg: scar tissue out of control. It's part of his medical history. If he were to donate sperm, he would have included that in the medical history section of his donor profile. Or would he? I list all of the things that are wrong with me that I don't even think of as part of my medical history: heart murmur, sensitive blood, the tendency to sneeze nonstop from August through October. Do donors think of all of these things: the odd allergies and ailments they are so used to that they don't even notice, the tendency for their scar tissue to congeal into strange mountainous protrusions, the great-uncle who is a kleptomaniac, the second cousin's athlete's foot?

Our mothers are excited. Faith's mother refers to my future biological child as her grandchild. My mother acknowledges that Faith will be mom number two. Our fathers wish us luck. It's all so easy. This is what we get for years of struggle for equality: mundane ordinariness. Acceptance. My sister already has mentioned throwing us a shower. We've come so far from the well of loneliness, from illicit sex and unrequited love, from lusting secretly after teachers, camp counselors, and college roommates. No more racing away from a family summer vacation to make out with a girl in a cabin two beach towns away. No more long walks in the woods with a woman whose hand casually brushes against yours "so you'll know." My mother calls to talk with Faith. Faith's sister offers me her maternity clothes. Sometimes I get bored.

In eighteen years not only will our donor potentially become a part of our lives, but so might our children's eight half-siblings (supposedly each donor is allowed to sire only ten children, assuming we take two of those slots...) and their families. Will the donor still be strapped for cash? Will he be met by a horde of nervous lesbians? Will he want our phone number? Will he want money? Will he leave us be? Will he even be alive?

Being a California donor means he has signed a waiver relinquishing all parental rights to the offspring his squirt might produce, and the state of California reinforces that waiver, would throw out of court any attempt on his part to locate me, us, supposedly. But everything changes. As we sign our forms of informed consent, the state of Oregon is in the process of revamping its once-concrete adoption laws. One of the arguments for a known donor had been, at least we know what the mess is rather than being met by a surprise mess later in life.

We put it all out of our minds. That is how we handle these issues. We file them away for eighteen years and nine months.

Even though we will try the first insemination at home, we register with a fertility center, just in case home insemination doesn't work and we need to have a doctor perform an intrauterine insemination. In order to register we are told we first must meet with a social worker to discuss our plans.

"No, no, no, you don't understand," I tell them. "We have been discussing this for years. We are both normal, healthy people who know how to make a decision."

Still they insist.

Listen, I say, I have been in therapy every year of my adult life except for two, and those were just a weird fluke. My mother is a psychoanalyst. My girlfriend's father is a psychiatrist. Even the father of our donor is a psychiatrist. We have been in couples counseling and have been discussing this for years. This is not some impulsive, sperm-of-the-moment thing. We are entirely aware of what we are getting into. We are in touch with our ambivalence as well as our rage (right now I am envisioning strangling the fucking social worker in a choke hold). We really don't need a forty-five minute (one-hundred-dollar) session with an idiot. It took me fifteen years to find a therapist I thought was smart enough to work with. And even if we had not spent the last few years of our relationship discussing whether or not to have a family and how to go about it, I highly doubt forty-five minutes with someone whose IQ is half my own would do a damn bit of good. If what you really want is another hundred bucks, then just tell me and I will give it to you rather than wasting our time as well as well as our money. By the way, if you don't make this same suggestion to your heterosexual clients, I am going to sue you until you are numb. Well, something like that.

It turns out their suggestion is, in fact, mandatory. And they have the best pregnancy record in town. So we meet with the social worker, whose only addition to our "process" is the phrase "biological adoption." As in, "Some people refer to conception with donor sperm as 'biological adoption.'" Thank you very much.

The next day the sperm bank offers us a free consultation with one of their "counselors," and I nearly lift my two-door Civic with one hand and toss it into the Charles River.

"We've already talked with a social worker." I withhold all the other things I'm thinking and want to say lest they retaliate by shipping us the seed of their new ex-convict summer intern instead of our kind Jew. "All we need to know, at this point, is how to do it. What to do with the sperm when it arrives."

"That's what the consultation is for," the woman says.

Oh.

Lesbian Civilization and Its Discontents

(ICE, BOMBS, AND ELLEN)

Our upstairs lesbian neighbors bring home their new "biologically adopted" baby. Phoebe is half Margaret and half donor number 4578, whose donor profile we looked up as soon as Margaret shared it with us (for the unspoken purpose of preventing us from selecting the same man). As I read about donor 4578's half-Jewish blond curls and brown eyes, my first thought is that he would be perfect for us. Donors are always greener on the other side of the fence. Now I hold the tiny girl in my arms and try to imagine those features that have nothing to do with Margaret melded with mine. What if I inseminated with donor 4578 anyway? Who is Margaret to tell us who can and cannot fertilize our eggs?

The idea of friends frequenting the same sperm banks introduces a whole new twist to the women-looking-for-men conundrum that has plagued females since the dawn of time, or at least since the first episode of *The Dating Game*. When discussing sperm donors with other lesbians, I often catch wind of a distinct and familiar rat that reminds me of college and high school, when girls fought over boys and even the most solid female friendships collapsed under the influence of a nice butt and a cleft chin. Here we are again, women choosing to spend their lives with other women but *still* willing to leap into the fire when it comes to catching a man and claiming his milky little genetics. Shouldn't we be light years away from fighting over sperm?

While the only other women in the world I should be negotiating genetic choice with are my sister and my mother, in the interest of proximity and immediate harmony, I acquiesce. Let Margaret and Beth have their donor. It would be too weird to raise children who were half sibs of their upstairs neighbors. Besides, there is Baldie and our $1,240 investment to consider.

Unfortunately, as the weeks of new motherhood pass, the power of Margaret's maternal instincts causes her to feel even more possessive of her child's biological father. She finally just comes out and says she doesn't want to share his seed—with anyone. She becomes overjoyed when she learns he has stopped donating, and gathers her finances in preparation for purchasing all of his deposits should he start up again. He is hers and hers alone, sent from heaven to stand in for her partner's missing machinery. One day we even hear her murmur, "Doesn't Phoebe have Beth's lips?" Faith and I smile silly little smiles that neither affirm nor deny the assertion and promise never ever to inseminate with number 4578.

But that is not enough. Soon after, Margaret suggests that all the procreating lesbians within a thirty-mile radius of our neighborhood share the numbers of their sperm donors so that everyone can be "aware" and not choose the same man.

It all seems fraught with disaster. Imagine the voice-mail: "Hey, you guys, just a heads up, Jennifer is really interested in donor number 8980, you know, because he's an Aries and she's a Leo. Anyway, sorry for the inconvenience. We knew you'd understand!"

I try to explain that one of the perks of being Lesbitarian is that we don't have to scratch each other's eyes out for a man. Besides, it's difficult enough to negotiate the choice of an anonymous donor with your partner—why would anyone want to open that decision up to another couple? And then who would get first dibs? It sounds like psychosocial quicksand. And then, of course, after you form this weekly potluck support group with every lesbian you know in order to avoid each choosing the same bio-dad, what happens but you are transferred to a new city and wind up buying a house next door to your kid's five half-sibs. Or your ten-year-old is in school and the new girl in his class is a half-sister who just moved here from Des Moines.

Part of the process of "biological adoption" is accepting how very bizarre it is, how strange and ultimately out of our control. Our kids will not have our partners' lips or eyes. They will have numerous half-sibs, some of whom might live three doors away. All you can do is suggest a blood test if your adult child chooses to shack up with a partner he or she too greatly resembles.

We tell Margaret we will not be participating in the sharing of donor ID numbers. The thought of having avoided women crying over plates of hummus and tabouli as they reveal all sorts of past privacies in an effort to plead their case for blue eyes over brown is like having avoided a major train wreck or been bypassed by a giant hurricane.

We are presented with yet another choice: dry ice or a nitrogen tank. Sperm is shipped to you in little vials that are kept frozen either by dry ice or by liquid nitrogen. "Nitrogen tank." I picture a scuba diver's heavy steel oxygen tank, a World War II vehicle, soldiers. We opt for dry ice. It's so much friendlier sounding, and at one hundred dollars per box, significantly cheaper. I can picture it, the sperm arriving on ice like shrimp cocktail or a frozen daiquiri, not encased in liquid nitrogen like nitroglycerin, like heart disease and bombs.

"That's hydrogen." The woman at the sperm bank must be a historian or physicist. She reminds me that dry ice is not like regular ice, not like the chips produced by my new Amana. Dry ice is special. You need to be wearing gloves when you touch it, and you can't get it at the supermarket. She goes on to warn us that a dry ice shipment is fraught with worry. You must continue to replenish the dry ice daily so that the specimen remains frozen. And though one can hardly fathom such an event, if Federal Express fails to deliver the sperm-on-ice cocktail in less than twenty-four hours, the dry ice will have melted and our frozen sperm will have become yesterday's baby. So unless you are absolutely, positively sure about your exact date of ovulation and one hundred percent confident in the country's number one courier, they—the sperm bank—suggest ordering your shipment in the nitrogen tank.

Okay! Okay! Give us the nitrogen bomb tank and the soldiers and take the extra sixty-five dollars from us.

The tank is scheduled to arrive at 10:30 next Wednesday

morning. The woman at the sperm bank swears it will be there by 10:30 and encourages me to stay home from work so that I can sign for it (a lost tank costs $1,000). That's two and a half hours late for work, one hundred and sixty-five dollars for the nitrogen bomb tank, one hundred and ninety-five dollars for each vial of ICI, yes-donor semen, plus the added effort of having to hunt down a Federal Express office where I can ship the tank back to the bank by Saturday morning, "at the latest." I figure she owes me a favor.

I ask her, "Do you know donor number 232?"

She pauses. In the three seconds the pause spans, I become convinced that yes, she does know our donor, and that the long pause is the sound of her struggle. Should she tell me that he is absolutely the ugliest, strangest, most mentally ill of all the donors she ever has met? But how could she after having shiested me the extra sixty-five dollars for the nitrogen bomb tank, having convinced me to miss two and a half hours of work? How does she break this awful news? I brace myself.

"No," she finally says. "He's from L.A."

L.A.?

During every phone conversation with the sperm bank—be it to order sperm, discuss shipment methods, give them my new credit card number, or report the date of my last period—I read between the lines. I pay careful, obsessive attention to every inflection, every pause, each word choice on the part of the sperm bank representative. I am convinced each one of them knows our donor, and though they can't tell us directly their opinion, they can hint. Maybe one of them even feels morally obligated to let us know how bad a choice we have made. *Wrong!*

Wrong! She wants to shout but can't, so instead pauses dramatically when I tell her what day of my cycle I am on, adds an incongruous chuckle after an exchange about syringes.

"They're trying to tell us something," I tell Faith. "Today the woman in charge of shipping sighed while we were talking about Federal Express."

I mourn the little Squirrel whose picture we saw, who had sound, albeit somewhat pathetic, reasons for donating semen, who would have produced very short but altruistic children without male pattern baldness. Instead we opted for a pictureless psychopath, from L.A., no less, city of tummy tucks and Botox and hair weaves.

"I've been on hold for five minutes. I think they're having a meeting about us."

Faith opens a beer. "The only genes I'm worried about are yours," she says.

She so doesn't get it.

Ellen and Anne broke up. I knew it. We all knew it. A tabloid says someone somewhere overheard Ellen, in a last-ditch effort to bring them back together, trying to convince Anne to have a baby.

I run into Beth and she dreamily says to me, "We're so-o-o different now." And I think to myself, I hope having a child never causes me to say things to my friends like, "We're so-o-o different now." But even more I hope I don't say, "Isn't he/she the most beautiful baby you've ever seen?" It is a quirk of evolution that programs every parent into thinking his or her baby is the most beautiful baby in the world so that he or she does not decide to eat it or leave it at the hospital. And I won't bring up breast-feeding unless somebody happens to asks me about it, and certainly not ever college funds, even if someone does happen to ask.

There is another pregnant lesbian among us. That makes three. It's like an epidemic.

Gay couples telling their childless friends they're going to try to get pregnant is like landing a one-two punch to the gut. In your thirties and forties, childless friends are hard to find. And their departure into parenthood can feel like a betrayal of sorts, a *There goes another one* kind of thing. I've felt it myself. Maybe that's what is so appealing about gay couples, the assumption that we will never change, that we are reliable and steady like your grandparents or an old unmarried aunt. When life gets complex there's always gay Yvonne or Queen David and their blissfully simple routine of work, travel, and a small cat or dog. But now we are as unpredictable and preoccupied as the next friend.

It's a Mad Mad Mad Mad Medical World

(Anxiety, Cancer, and All Roads in Between)

I worry about my surges of anxiety, about how the wave of panic that encompasses me will affect my unborn child, should I ever have an unborn child taking up residence inside me. Since my mother's diagnosis four years ago of ovarian cancer, there have been these moments, really horrible moments, in which we are waiting for the results of a blood test or waiting for a doctor's call or waiting for my mother to come out of surgery. And when the call comes or the results are in or the surgeon happens to appear two hours early from surgery, my body seizes. My entire being becomes fear and I rush to the bathroom or sit down and stare into space. It's manageable enough, though barely, when it's just me alone living in this body, when I can talk myself through the chemistry. But what about a fetus? What about a fetus with no understanding of the world or anything else except that suddenly and without warning life is filled with tremendous blood-curdling fear?

And then, at my most narcissistic and evil, I worry that there are toxins at the Dana-Farber Cancer Institute, where I take my mother for her monthly chemotherapy treatments. I wonder whether cancer researchers intentionally pollute the drinking water and cafeteria food with carcinogens in order to continue the epidemic and keep themselves afloat. Cancer is big business after all, and maybe all that talk about genetics and familial history really reflects the fact that family members caring for a person with cancer are being exposed to cancer-causing agents at clinics across America.

I would never suspect a European nation of doing such a thing. It's paranoid and crazy, something to do with a dreaded loss of control and feelings about my mother. I vow never to confess these thoughts to a single soul.

I'm visiting my mother after the third treatment of her third round of chemotherapy when my uncle, her brother, who has flown to Boston from Michigan to take care of her, tells me it is a myth that male pattern baldness is passed down the mother chain.

"Who told you that?!" I could kill him, this kind man.

"A dermatologist."

Shit. Shit, shit, shit. We will have little bald sons and it's all my fault—not my father's, but my own. For believing folklore. For caring too much about other things like medical history and brains, like Judaism and whether our bald sons can meet their bald father one day when they are eighteen years old. Ask any eighteen-year-old male which he would prefer, a head of hair or a meeting with a guy who jerked off into a cup, and then tell me not to worry.

Because I'm temporarily preoccupied with genetics, entirely self-absorbed with the overwhelming responsibility of mating my genes, I fail to remember that baldness is a loaded topic here in my mother's home. Baldness isn't just some annoying little genetic bummer. Baldness is what happens when you have cancer and must undergo chemotherapy. Baldness is my mother's biggest nemesis, second only to her own mortality. Five-foot-seven, sophisticated and elegant in her designer clothing and handmade jewelry, my mother once sported the thickest head of brown curls known to our family. Nowadays, when she is not entirely bald, her hair is fine and limp, a wilted reminder of the spiritual and physical toll the cancer has taken.

If we have a bald son, I will count my blessings that I have a child, and that we, hopefully, are present and healthy enough to argue the point of male-pattern baldness. I apologize to my mother for my lack of sensitivity by simply dropping the subject and making us all some lunch.

I have a dream that the sperm bank sends, along with the two ICI vials due next week, a copy of our donor's long form free of charge. Oh, my God, that's so nice, I think in my dream; usually they cost an extra twenty dollars. And then I read it and our bald drag queen has written all sorts of funny things about which numbers he prefers. They have asked him what his favorite number is, and he has written a long paragraph about liking the numbers zero and nine and three because they have curves. And in my dream I think, he has such a great sense of humor! And I'm so relieved. Relieved enough to reread his statement on why he has chosen to donate sperm, and it too is beautiful and witty. In my dream I am so happy and

pleased with myself for having picked the right guy.
There's nothing to worry about after all.

I dream about the tank. And in the dream, sure enough,
it's huge and foreboding. I dream about the semen. And it's
thick and grainy and gray, like the grapefruit seed facial
scrub I bought a couple of weeks ago. I smear it inside my
vagina and on my cervix and wait.

My mother tells me, after I spend the day taking her for
a chemo session, buying her groceries, cleaning up from
dinner, that I should be pampered this week, the countdown
to insemination number one.

"Pampered?"

"Look at you. You don't even know what that means."

The next night Faith takes me out for dinner. I assume
it's a way of pampering me and that I should do nothing
more but lean back and relax. But after we're done eating, I have this bizarre auditory experience that turns out
to be a kind of anxiety attack in which the clinking of
forks on plates seems weirdly close to me and in my head,
even though, apparently, it is coming from across the
room. I tell Faith I am hearing clinking sounds and she
says the acoustics are weird, that the room is so big that
the clinking from other people's plates sounds like it's
coming from my lap. We're surrounded by parents and
children because we've intentionally chosen to eat at a
family restaurant, like traveling to another country to
observe the culture.

The clinking comes again, and I start to panic. I think
maybe I'm not hearing well from my left ear. I go pale. I'm
convinced I've left my body, that my soul's floated up to the

dusty ceiling while my corpse remains blank and dumb at our little gay table for two. I'm either tripping or have West Nile Virus.

Faith says, "You're not going to go crazy, are you?"

But I already am. I think I might have to ask her to help me stand, to guide me from our little table to the front door. I talk very slowly and clearly and convince myself I am all right enough to walk. In the car I picture myself at home, free to freak out even more, free to indulge in this panic.

"Let's go to a movie."

The screen totally distracts me from myself, from my mother's cancer, and from pending pregnancy, and I am fine.

The rest of that weekend is oddly beautiful and peaceful. The August air is gray and cool. Faith and I go for a walk. We drag home a small red Adirondack chair from someone's garbage. She plays piano and I paint. Friends come over and we soak chunks of two-by-fours in a bucket of water, throw them on coals, and smoke a chicken. Faith and I hold each other close. Our days are numbered. I think that's what's going on. That and the gift of a cool, gray summer day.

Today is Monday. The nitrogen bomb tank arrives in ten days. I dream I open the tank and remove a vial of semen to look it over, but then I forget to return it to the tank and it goes bad. Just like that. Hundreds of dollars down the drain. No insemination. No pregnancy. I'm disappointed. Thank goodness.

I am afraid of miscarriage. Afraid of having a damaged child. Afraid of not getting pregnant. Afraid of babies. Afraid of childbirth. Afraid of fear.

I have a deep, dark secret. I once spent three years preparing for medical school, taking classes, applying. I was accepted and then freaked out because all along something in me had known I didn't really want to go. Maybe I believed I wouldn't really get in, or that once I did get in I would be different somehow, changed. One-minded. Directed. Certain of my medical—or nonmedical—path. Much to my chagrin, when I was accepted I was still the same person and thus was left scrambling for a way to know what to do. So I deferred my acceptance and moved away, fell in love, quit my job, started it again, meditated, practiced Reiki, wrote, prayed. A year and a half later, when I was no closer to an answer, I fired my brain, told it to shut up or go away. I told myself that at 8:30 on Monday morning I would know what I wanted to do by virtue of where I found myself. If I was in Anatomy Lab with my bone box and cadaver, then I would be a medical student. If not…

At 8:30 A.M. I was sitting by a pond watching a cormorant perched on the side of a rowboat dry its wings. My mind crept in to see if I was in trouble, if I was going to be punished or arrested. But there I was, the decision made.

I am doing that now, following my heart, going forth despite the orchestra of chaos and confusion conducted by the incessant bandleader in my brain, my overactive mind. Going ahead, following my heart, buying sperm and moving ahead despite the deafening symphony of anxiety and strange dreams and somatic symptoms, going ahead against my own will, it sometimes seems. Groping blindly, as if my eyes are closed and I don't have the sense enough to open them.

My sister's doctor convinces my sister to convince our mother to have a blood test to determine whether or not she carries the Ashkenazi Jewish gene for cancer, i.e., whether my sister and I are at risk for developing a host of reproductive cancers and whether we will be passing down this potential death sentence to each of our offspring. Apparently, my anxiety level has not been high enough these last few weeks, and our guardian angels arrange for the results of the genetic test to be delivered to my mother and me while we sit in the tenth-floor infusion room of the Dana-Farber Cancer Institute during round three, number three of my mother's treatment for ovarian cancer, and six days before I am due to inseminate for the first time. Hooray for science.

"You're really going to like Sue," my mother says of the genetic counselor who will be delivering our fate.

I can't imagine liking Sue. I can't imagine thinking, as my mother is filled with lifesaving poison, "Wow. What a really neat woman. I wonder if you can invite your genetic counselor out for dinner?"

When we see Sue at the nurses' station, my mother smiles and cheerfully shouts across the room, "Over here!"

Sue is accompanied by a doctor. I find this ominous, but my happy-go-lucky mother informs me, "It's just part of the study."

"We're part of a study?"

My mother introduces me to Sue and the doctor and everyone is smiling because we're all one big happy family and it's like a wedding or a bar mitzvah, only I have that feeling that I get whenever we're at the hospital and a doctor approaches us to give us some new information. It's like a tingling sensation times a thousand, like plugging yourself into a light socket or eating seven pounds of MSG, like a wicked major "uh-oh."

"Well," Sue says, and pauses.

Now it's the Academy Awards.

"I have good news."

My mother, it turns out, does not carry any genetic mutations predisposing her to Jewish cancer.

"Oh, that's wonderful!" she says. "I'm good. I'm good." As if she would have been bad. "I didn't want to do that to you girls." As if it would have been her fault.

"There's nothing to worry about," Sue chirps.

"Except that we're here anyway," I say, and look at the doctor who nods her head, and finally, at long last, everybody stops smiling.

With four days to go before insemination I decide to try Japanese acupuncture. My overt intention is to enhance my fertility, but secretly I'm hoping to change my life, to become a more patient and compassionate person, to become more disciplined and maybe have thicker hair.

The difference between Chinese acupuncture and Japanese acupuncture is enormous. As far as I can tell from my brief encounter with each, Chinese acupuncture involves a large needle the size of ruler that is inserted into a very tender "spot" until it hurts, and Japanese acupuncture involves a small, flexible needle, almost a filament or a hair, that is inserted without your knowing it is there; you can even leave it taped in place for days at a time.

At my first Japanese session a very empathic woman named Martha spends an hour asking me all sorts of questions about my medical history. After that she lays me down and inserts little needle hairs in my ankles and wrists, and along my "conception meridian." Then she dims the lights and leaves me alone for ten long minutes to relax and come in touch with my maternal self.

I figure I should meditate, follow my breath in and out, and really let my body open to the needle hairs and the idea of motherhood. Instead I wonder about the evolutionary purpose of homosexuality. If being gay serves a function—say, limits the population of a species—then what does it mean that lesbians are procreating? Are we screwing with the natural order? Should we be living like those lone wolves that never reproduce but instead help raise the children of their siblings? After all, that would be the next best thing to getting one's genes into the next generation.

Martha peeks her head in to see how I am.

"Fine," I tell her. Though I seem to have developed a persistent sharp pain in my left ankle.

"Your kidney," Martha tells me, triumphant. "There must have been a block."

To distract myself from the pain I try to guess how much money Ellen DeGeneres has. I wonder how much she made on her HBO special. Is she worth two million dollars or more? Less? And who would make more on a movie nowadays, her or Anne Heche? Were they actually struggling financially as an article in some magazine suggested? I thought Anne was far too skinny to get pregnant. She's so skinny—I don't think I would want to hug her, maybe just shake her hand. I would hug Ellen DeGeneres. And I would hug Lily Tomlin, but not Jane Wagner. I consider that perhaps in all relationships—gay or straight—there is one party you would want to hug and one you would not. I wonder which category I belong to.

Martha returns to remove the needle hairs. "Were you able to relax?"

"Yes."

She decides to leave the needle hairs in my ears. "They're in your Valium points," she says with a smile.

Very funny.

I'm instructed to leave them in for five days.

The Soldiers Are at the Door

(Speculums, Syringes, and New Jersey)

The nitrogen tank containing the first sperm of the rest of our lives arrives the day after tomorrow. People who know about it ask if we're going to "light candles." What they really want to know is whether the insertion of said semen will be a sexual experience, whether I will have an orgasm to facilitate the transport of anonymous semen up through my cervix and onward ho! into my uterus—peristaltic love waves rushing the expensive XY to my XX.

I imagine it will go like this instead: My alarm will go off at 7 A.M., at which point I will pee on a stick to see if I'm ovulating. If so, I will remove a vial from the tank and set it out to thaw for a half-hour. When Faith wakes up at 7:30 she will be instructed to carefully fill the syringe. "Wait," she will say. "I have to go to the bathroom." She then will go into the bathroom and close the door for what will feel like an hour and a half. Then she will want to grind beans and start brewing a pot of coffee, so that by the time she is done with the injection and perhaps a few peristaltic waves, her coffee will be ready. I likely will stand over her worrying that she doesn't know how to retract fluid into a syringe, worried she will spill, worried she won't inject the syringe far enough inside me. I will get anxious. Faith will get mad. And then we will have a fight.

"Maybe we should stretch out my vagina." I'm thinking that years without a man's engorged member inside me may have caused my vaginal opening to shrink to the size of a small ring of calamari, not nearly large enough for an entire baby to push its way through.

"A speculum," Faith suggests. We could stretch me open bit by bit over the next few months if only we had our very own speculum, something we assume works much like a tire jack. *Ratchet, ratchet,* one night. *Ratchet, ratchet, ratchet* the next.

We wonder about Jennifer, a lesbian friend who has had a baby but has never had sex with a man. Is she a virgin? Was it an immaculate conception? If the definition of immaculate conception is a woman becoming pregnant without having had intercourse with a man, well, then, the times really are a-changin'.

My first cousin is marrying a Catholic woman who insists on baptizing their future children and who refuses to allow the Hora to be played at their wedding. His father, my uncle, is up in arms. Mothers and stepmothers and old great aunts are converging to dissect the relationship, to try to figure out just what went wrong and where. How *could* he? What could he possibly see in a shiksa who hates the Hora?

"It's ironic, isn't it?" I tell them when they call the two Jewish future lesbian moms to talk about it. "Isn't it ironic?"

Simone's mother, my best friend, Tory, delivers to our door a two-foot-tall fertility goddess. The goddess is all dark wood and breasts, and I am strangely attracted to her. I carry her into the bedroom and plant her on an old wicker dresser. The next day I am inspired to go out and buy a night table just so she will feel at home, special. I spend three hours assembling the night table and then gently offer it to the goddess. She accepts, and soon her dark body stands in stark contrast to the white wooden Crate and Barrel sale item that is now her pedestal. Apparently, two couples have gotten pregnant in no more than three tries with this goddess in their bedroom. I feel fertile just looking at her. I feel moist and voluptuous and ripe. Pretending to adjust her position, I steal a feel of her breasts, her thighs. She is stoic. Beyond lust. She is all about birth with a capital earth. I am nervous around her. I fear she is more of a woman than I could ever be. She accepts the size of her breasts, the fullness of her hips and mouth as divine. She is vessel, open and almighty. I slouch and wear baggy clothes. I am wet sponge, afraid and ambivalent.

That evening, after spending way too much time staring at and stroking the fertility goddess, I tell Faith, "I think I'm pregnant from just having bought sperm. That goddess did it."

"What goddess?"

"The one on the new night table in the bedroom."

"We have a new night table?"

In the past week I have had two dreams in which Faith was having an affair. In each dream she was sleeping with an obese woman. In one dream they just kissed. In the other they had sex, and I was so mad I told Faith to sleep in another room until we decided which one of us would move out.

Perhaps the oddest thing about choosing an anonymous sperm donor and inseminating, if you are as loose-lipped as the two of us, is that everyone knows you're doing it.

"I'll be thinking of you on Thursday!"

I remind these well-intentioned people that insemination only takes us to the starting line, the place where most other couples begin. Still, there is this sense that we have paid our infertility dues, that by virtue of having to pay for sperm and then have it injected into you you somehow are exonerated from miscarriages, ectopic pregnancies, or an inability to conceive. Like you get one hurdle or another, not all of them.

The nitrogen bomb tank filled with semen is due to arrive by 10:30 A.M. Wednesday, day eleven of my incredibly regular cycle, but it never arrives. The tank never comes. I get up at 7 and nervously occupy myself with cleaning, showering, cleaning, checking E-mail, cleaning, until 10:33, when I consider calling the police, a lawyer, and *The New York Times*. I can't call the sperm bank because it is 7:33 A.M. in California and they're closed for another hour and a half, or perhaps forever, as I imagine they have gone out of business, taking my money and semen with them. I wait another fifteen minutes. It occurs to me that the sperm bank is a front, a hoax like those men who prey on widows by pretending to be rich and available. The women have taken our credit card number and the copy of our signatures and gone off to South America to gamble. Or maybe they've been shut down due to allegations that the director, Dr. Big Dick, has been selling his own ejaculate to unsuspecting women for the last twenty-five years and is figured to have sired 10,382 babies.

Worse than either of these two reasons is the possibility that someone screwed up. That thought makes me crazy. I will bring them down. I will take them out. I will ruin them just as they have ruined my chances to conceive this month, just as they have dictated the course of my future by forcing one egg over another. What doesn't occur to me is the weather, the fact that it is dark as night this morning and pelting rain so loud and hard it sounds as if someone is throwing nitrogen tanks at the house.

"I have some bad news," the woman at the sperm bank says when I finally reach her at 9:01 A.M. Pacific time. "The connecting flight was canceled due to weather. Your tank is in New Jersey."

Jersey?

I have to admit the fact that the nitrogen bomb tank is in New Jersey is oddly comforting because Jersey is my home state and therefore most of my own genetic material (in the form of cousins and aunts and uncles) is also in New Jersey. That, and the grandmother whose death taught me that one must procreate in order to maintain the wonder of unconditional love, in order to survive the loss of our elders, the grandmother I plan on naming a child after, was from New Jersey. So the tank being in Jersey is strangely normal.

The adequately remorseful woman at the sperm bank says the tank is scheduled to arrive in Boston tomorrow. The moral of the story: Request your sperm a day early, bombs not ice.

It's here! The armored nitrogen bomb tank and all of the soldiers are at our door by 10 A.M., and suddenly I believe in miracles. In good men who donate sperm for good reasons. In sperm banks that make money, yes, but get lesbians and infertile heterosexuals pregnant. In girlfriends who when put to the test will not spill. I want to inseminate now! But I am not ovulating as expected, and Faith is not home. So I remove the deep, dark fertility goddess from her Crate and Barrel pedestal, plant her on top of the tank, and drive to work.

In the car I realize I have huge feelings for the tank. I can only imagine how a mother must feel about a child or a pregnant woman about the life she is carrying inside her if this is how I feel about a nitrogen tank—somebody else's nitrogen tank no less, one I have to return in no more than four days lest I be charged $1,000. But in this tank is my baby, or at least the rest of the cards necessary to play my hand at motherhood. I feel proud of the tank. Proud of myself. Proud of Faith. Proud of us for coming so far despite gnawing ambivalence and fear.

When I get home from work and look at the tank I am filled with terror and want to throw up.

Duh! Just because a person is not ovulating in the morning does not mean she will not be ovulating in the evening. This from Faith, due to arrive home in two hours. The ovulation kit says make sure you haven't had anything to eat in the two hours prior to testing. Not eating is easy when you're asleep, but if you're awake and nervous, waiting for your girlfriend to come home from work so you can pee on the stick and then open the scary tank, pull out a stranger's semen, and squirt it into you, then it's hell. No eating. No drinking. And I can't take a bath because supposedly that isn't a good thing to do when you're pregnant and even though I'm not, I could be soon and wouldn't want my basal body temperature raised to the point of overheating my uterus and cooking my unborn child. Masturbation is out because I need to save my peristaltic waves for later. Reading is absolutely out of the question as that requires presence of mind and the ability to focus on something other than myself. There is nothing else to do but dress up the tank. I return the fertility goddess to her pedestal and in her place rest Faith's favorite hat. I wrap one of her shirts around the tank and prop her glasses beneath the hat, and voilà! It's her, and the sperm is hers, and we're one big normal family!

I remember Unibrow and how his coloring most closely matched my girlfriend's, and have a twinge—okay, a gut-wrenching jab—of regret. I remember, because I am that way, all of them—the Navajo, Big Jew, Giant Jew, the Squirrel—and think how bizarre it is that a decision so flip and so based on superficial nothings will wind up creating a child who will feel inevitable and born of fate, not choice or availability, not because of eyebrows or height. But conception is all the time random and arbitrary—a zillion sperm, January's egg instead of December's because you had a business trip. We are all here but for the grace of God and one moment's decision over another.

Because this must be why it was invented, once the tank is dressed I turn on the television.

Doing It!

(Isn't It Romantic Take One, Sex, and Chicken)

I picture a man and a woman deciding it's time to try to become pregnant. They go out for a special dinner, come home, and glide into their bedroom. For the first time she isn't taking the pill or he isn't using a condom or the diaphragm has been thrown in the kitchen trash along with empty cat food cans and wilted parsley. They are going to do it unhindered. They're going to make a baby. He whips off his shirt, unzips his fly, and thrusts his manhood in and out, in and out, as she lies back in full lordosis already making the list of invites for the shower.

And then there is us.

The late-night ovulation test reads SURGE! Just as Faith predicted.

"Let's do it!" she roars.

Come on team, play ball!

Faith reads aloud the instruction sheet that has come with the nitrogen tank as I, donning a pair of winter gloves in the dead of a steamy August, carefully unlock the tank. Inside is another tank, even more ominous-looking. On the lid of the inner tank a label reads DO NOT SCREW. A cruel joke.

"Lift the lid off the inner tank," Faith reads in a frightened whisper.

I'm a member of a bomb squad, hunched over in my gloves and shorts, carefully, slowly removing the lid. It slides off with a rush of freezing steam and I leap back. Faith gasps. It's *The X-Files* and *If These Walls Could Talk 2* rolled into one.

There are no instructions as to what to do with the smoking lid and the long Styrofoam rod that is attached to it once they are removed. Faith is afraid to touch it. Can it go on the floor or a rug without burning a hole through the foundation of our house? I decide to keep the lid in my left hand as with my trembling right I awkwardly pull a long metal stick up and out of the smoking caldron. The metal stick is like a ladle that scoops up for us the infamous "cane." I've heard about this cane before. It's the rod that holds the vials. I pictured the cane to be similar to an old man's walking stick, only creepier, with frightening images carved into it and a lethal tip. But this cane is simply a long metal rod in which are lodged four very expensive little plastic vials.

Four?

"Didn't we buy two vials?"

Faith reads a note that has come attached to our instructions. It says, in brief, that we have received four vials instead of two as the motility of our donor's sperm was lower in this sample than the bank would have liked.

"It's fine," Faith interrupts the tirade forming in my head: Are two mediocre vials better than one excellent vial? Is there something wrong with our donor? Should we stop right now and demand our money back? New vials? But I want so much to try that when Faith says, "Let's go," I trust her inherently. She is a scientist now, not a musician.

I try to remove two vials from the cane but can't. They won't budge. The four vials of half-assed sperm are permanently cemented to the cane.

"Read to me how to remove them," I tell Faith through gritted teeth.

Strangely, there are no instructions for how to remove the vials. There are instructions for everything else except this majorly crucial step in the journey to parenthood.

Still clutching the lid in my other hand, I try to force one out. No luck. I worry the whole batch is melting, going bad before our eyes. I yank. I twist.

"Don't twist!"

"That's screw. Don't *screw* the lid."

Finally I whip the lid onto the floor (there is no hole sonically burned through even to the basement, just a small bit of condensation) and manage to pry one vial and then another out of the cane. I quickly send the cane and the remaining vials back down into the smoking vat, replace the lid—without screwing—then clamp closed the larger outer tank and look over at Faith. We are paralyzed, already exhausted.

Next we have to thaw the vials. This is such a big deal. You're supposed to put the vials in a baggie and then submerge the baggie in a bowl of warm—NOT HOT!—water. If the water is too hot the sperm will die. It is way too much for me, an obsessive, to bear, deciding on the perfect temperature of tap water. I just can't do it. Our other option is to let the vials sit for a while at room temperature. Even though it's 11 P.M., I opt for the sitting. I would rather stay awake all night waiting for the semen to thaw than risk cooking it.

With a heavy sigh Faith grabs the vials from me, shoves them in a baggie, runs water to a perfect "warm," and submerges the baggie.

"You want some chicken?" she asks.

The brave scientist, not yet having had a chance to have dinner, pulls a half-eaten chicken from the refrigerator and dives in.

"It's a special night...you could put it on a plate," I tell her.

I pace, checking the little vials over and over again until at last they no longer are encased in ice and each vial is revealed to contain one milliliter of opaque yellow liquid.

I don't remember semen being yellow. But then I never poured it into a vial, froze it for ten months, then thawed it in a baggie. It's a strange thing, this yellow liquid, the bodily fluid of a stranger. What was he thinking when he shot this wad? Is he somewhere now wondering about his sperm? Is he at this very moment wondering if a woman somewhere is inseminating with his seed? Well, we are! Here we are in Boston, and we are!

Faith puts the chicken back in the refrigerator and then it's back to the bedroom. No, first to the living room to get pillows. No, wait, to the bathroom to pee so I won't have to get up for two hours (two hours is the amount of time the sperm bank recommends a woman spend lying down in various conception-enhancing positions after insemination). Pee. Get the pillows with which to prop my pelvis. Back to the bedroom and then...strip. So unceremonious it all is. I whip off my clothes and lie back in wait.

Faith's job is to remove the syringe from the package, carefully, without spilling, unscrew (this time we can) the cap from the vial, place the syringe in the vial all the way to the bottom, and slowly retract the yellow liquid. Once the syringe is full, she is to make sure the precious seed doesn't dribble out the end of the syringe before she quickly places it in my vagina. I watch as she tears open the package containing the syringe.

"You have chicken on your face."

"Shit."

Faith races into the bathroom to wash her face. Upon returning sparkling clean, she carefully removes the syringe, gently unscrews the vial, brilliantly determines there is a cap on the syringe that must be removed, fills the syringe without spilling, and...ten minutes after we have slowly inserted and retracted both vials I think I feel something moving inside me.

"I'm pregnant!"

Then I get anxious. The incredible hugeness of what we're doing hits and surprises me, as if all along I had thought we were buying a car. And there's no turning back. It's perhaps the biggest, most life-altering, most irreversible thing you can do, and here I've been joking about it, writing it all down, treating it like just another thing. Faith starts to do a fertility chant in the direction of my womb and I think, whoa, let's not get carried away. Maybe I don't want this to happen so soon.

At night I dream I'm visiting my old elementary school. I'm dropping in on different classes to see what it would be like to teach older kids, younger kids. The older kids make me nervous, as if I were a peer among them, so I go down the stairs, past the cafeteria, to the lower school. In an empty kindergarten classroom a young teacher is setting up for her class. She's listening to a CD of a man singing and playing guitar. I think what a great place to teach, to work, to spend my time. Except I find that the room opens up to a train track, and suddenly it all seems so dangerous.

The next morning we repeat the procedure despite my protests that I most certainly am already pregnant, and if not no longer really want to be anyway, so what's the point. Later in the day my stomach feels bloated and I suffer cramps that will last the next two weeks.

For the time being we are free. No more ovulation kits, no more nitrogen bomb tanks that cost one hundred sixty-five dollars, not including sperm, and then wind up in New Jersey. We simply wait. Part of me wishes there had been candles, more ritual, not Faith leaving me splayed with a syringe poking out of my vagina (the syringe is supposed to stay in for twenty minutes so that every last bit of semen makes it inside you) while she flossed and brushed her teeth in preparation for the peristaltic waves.

Afterward, I smelled the syringe and could smell the semen. When it leaked out of me I smelled it again. It smelled good, clean, healthy, kind. They say attraction is all about smell. Hopefully the man whose genetic material I'm carrying is someone I'd at least find attractive enough to have lunch with. His semen certainly wasn't offensive in the least. At one point I even thought I smelled cologne.

Three days after our insemination I bleed. There's a

small but noticeable amount of blood in my discharge and some bloody tissue type of thing in the toilet. I decide it is an embryo that failed to implant passing through me, and I am so sad that I cry all the way to Provincetown, a two-and-a-half-hour car ride from Boston to the tip of Cape Cod, and the sadness is such a relief because mostly I haven't been wanting to be pregnant. I know it's insane to be trying and afraid all at the same time. It's not like I would abort or anything if it works.

It's just that I am terrified.

Why Did the Pilgrims Leave Provincetown for Plymouth Rock?

ANSWER: .LAVINRAC GNIRUD KRAP
OT ECALP A DNIF T'NDLUOC YEHT

We're in Provincetown for a week, staying with my mother in a small cottage as she paints and recovers from chemotherapy and I obsess over whether I'm pregnant. Everyone is treating me very tenderly, making sure I don't lift anything too heavy and that I eat enough breakfast—until I tell them about the bloody tissuey thing. And though they reassure me it's too soon for anything to happen, they suddenly start asking me to load firewood into the car, to take the dog for a walk.

My mother is doing well, though the risk of this new chemo is that it can cause blistering lesions on her hands and feet and inside her mouth. She always says she's fine but I notice she hasn't been in the water this year and is hardly walking through town. Her cancer is a good distraction from my potential pregnancy, and my potential pregnancy is a good distraction from her cancer. It gets even weirder if you think about her cancer beginning in her ovaries and about

74

pregnancy as a journey that also begins there. Right now my mother's hands and feet burn sometimes, but there are no lesions. She puts moisturizer in the refrigerator so it will feel cool when she applies it, as the doctor told her to do in an effort to ward off the lesions. She makes us dinner every night, buys all the groceries, is paying for the cottage. I am a child here, and so the thought of being a parent is distressing, giving up my own childhood in a way. And could I ever provide this for my own children? A week on the beach? Or will we have to send them to some summer Massachusetts youth league where they mow grass from median strips and pick up garbage alongside the highway? The cramps that preceded the passage of bloody tissue are gone, so I'm even more convinced I'm not pregnant. I could call a doctor, but a vacation for my family means a vacation from doctors.

My mother has a blister on her foot. We all play it off: "Oh, it's so small. Don't worry." But inside, at least inside me, there is terror. In the cancer club, while you dread the treatment, you dread even more not being able to get or tolerate the treatment.

Not only do I feel less pregnant than ever, but after visiting friends with two children, ages three and five, I'm absolutely certain I don't want a child. At our peaceful cottage, where we each get to sleep in every morning, I'm reassured by my mother and Faith that I will feel different about our own children, that their screaming and shouting will be trying but wonderful.

"Yeah, right."

"Imagine my life without you," my mother says.

I think that is perhaps the motivation at the heart of the matter, to someday have a thirty-year-old we can rely on. Such a fragile, wrong reason to have a child when you consider that life is so unpredictable, children so much their own individuals. A terrible twist of fate can occur, or a child can grow into an adult who just doesn't care.

A Buddhist friend of mine says you must choose parenthood for present reasons, as opposed to making decisions based on an unknown future, on something that doesn't even exist. But some of us, like myself, if left to the present would never initiate change. I'd still be living in my childhood bedroom in New Jersey. My parents would still be tucking me in and making the rules. It is precisely these imagined un-Zen leaps into fantasy that propel me to shake things up, to ultimately change, if not in the way I had foreseen, then in some other manner. Equilibrium is quiet and nice, but where does it lead? At the end of my life will I be more grateful for a life of restaurants, movies, and sleep-filled nights or for bold risks and those scattered leaps of faith that have brought to my life a companion, a child, a mortgage?

The blister has shrunk. Hopefully the cancer has too.

My cramps are becoming more consistent. In a moment of apparent calm, the phrase *tubal pregnancy* pops into my head and I freak. My heart races and I become terrified with the certainty that all this—these cramps, the spotting—is a precursor to a tubal pregnancy. A friend of mine who has survived four miscarriages and the birth of a healthy baby boy reassures me I am crazy. Maybe you're pregnant. Maybe I'm pregnant? How could I be pregnant? I haven't had sex with a man in more than ten years. It's like part of me still doesn't believe what we've done.

In a dream a beautiful blond-haired boy comes to see me to say hello. He will be my son. He has just popped into this dream to tell me, to introduce himself. He is smiling and excited. We're going to have so much fun together.

It is Tuesday. On Friday, either I menstruate or I don't. On Friday, we also find out whether this new round of chemotherapy is successfully beating back my mother's cancer. That is just too much for one day. I wish there were some way to change it all, to spread it out, so that one is not forever linked with the other.

More than the fear that comes with a report from an oncologist, I dread sorrow. I can handle rage and anticipation, but the dull thud of bad news, the life-will-never-be-the-same end of hope—that really sucks. I know what it means to bring a baby into a world of sorrow. When my mother's father died suddenly at age fifty-eight, a year after my parents were married, my mother impulsively decided to get pregnant. Rather than wait a year as had been the plan, she decided to distract herself from heartbreak with a baby, decided to fight death with life. It is not lost on me the similarity, that I—the baby born of sorrow—somehow am doing the same thing. But I am thirty-nine, the cancer four and a half years old. Life has to go on. Still.

Back to the City

(Isn't It Romantic Takes Two and Three)

It's Thursday.

Each morning I perform a pregnancy test, because I can. I take them by the handful from the hospital where I work, stash them in our linen closet, pee in a Dixie cup first thing in the morning, and stare at the emerging single line like it's a Polaroid. The results always are negative. Each time I'm a little disappointed—and a little relieved. It's like an emotional rehearsal. I don't tell anyone about it, lest they think me wasteful or a thief or barren or crazy. *Barren.* Now there's a word. *Barren women.* So much of medical terminology is misogynist or just downright stupid. *Incompetent cervix. Inadequate uterus. Successful suicide.* These are the longest two weeks of my life. At least I haven't had to clean the litter box.

On day twenty-six my period is not a day early. On day twenty-seven my period is not on time. In the afternoon of day twenty-eight I am officially a half-day late. By the end of day twenty-eight I have menstrual cramps and am bleeding. Faith and I are both so sad and disappointed, and that is our gift. Even better perhaps than becoming pregnant on the first try is the gift of knowing we are doing the right thing, that we do indeed want this overwhelming and terrifying thing to happen. We count off twelve days until we can try again. IUI with a doctor. I will miss the tank and our night of sexual science. I will be nostalgic for us and our brave first steps.

In the meantime I become a self-centered hedonist indulging in all of life's sinful treats. I am a woman without a child. I stay up late and get up late. I drink margaritas and glasses of wine, run every day too fast and too long, and eat raw oysters. I spend money on myself and consider an overseas trip. Overall, I take about twenty-seven giant steps away from the scaled mountain of my ambivalence. I'm back below tree level, sucking in oxygen like there's no tomorrow.

And then I learn there's a chance that the sperm bank will not release our next vial in time for me to inseminate in two weeks, and I replace my pack, drop my goblet, and trudge upward, calculating my expected ovulation date to the minute, negotiating with the sperm bank until it's settled: one IUI vial to be delivered to my doctor in another nitrogen bomb tank in time for me to try again.

The IUI takes three minutes tops. It is the most anticlimactic event of my life. Afterward, Faith and I hug each other and she goes home to rehearse with the band and I go back to work. I don't think I feel anything moving inside me. I don't have a moment of panic. In my mind it's an event unassociated with pregnancy or parenthood. It's a pap smear or an oil change. I call Faith a few hours later.

"Why haven't you checked in?"

Same reason. It's just sort of a nonevent, small in comparison to the rest of the week's anticipation of it. I wonder if this time I might even forget to do a pregnancy test.

I return to the doctor for a physical. I figure it's my duty as a potential vessel to make sure all systems are functioning properly. A new doctor greets me with a handshake. She's a huge heterosexual palomino with long blond hair and a diamond engagement ring the size of a Volkswagen. I sigh at the thought of coming out, of telling this fertile heterosexual with her own live-in white-collar sperm bank about trying to get pregnant via dysfunctional sperm. When I do, she blinks. And then we proceed. I give her a 7.5, maybe even 7.9, which is as close as you get to a perfect physical when you are not the president of the United States or Madonna. If I was the president, or even an ex-president, I'd be hospitalized overnight and scheduled to undergo all sorts of testing and probing—stress tests, sigmoidoscopies, mole searches. Instead I have a very thorough proletariat physical and then it's back out to join the workers. I imagine my HMO requiring me to give birth in a field. At least we have figured out what's wrong with my finger: temporary post-traumatic arthritis. At least she did a breast exam and checked my pulse.

This waiting is different. This waiting is expensive. I begin the calculations in my head before bed, at work when I should be doing other things. I figure this process of trying to get pregnant via an anonymous sperm donor is costing us six hundred dollars a month. How long is it before a child costs you six hundred dollars a month? My friend Tory's daughter, Simone, is in preschool for three hundred dollars a month. Clothing can be expensive but can always be purchased secondhand. So, wondering whether or not I am pregnant now also involves wondering how we can continue to afford six hundred dollars a month. I consider quitting therapy for a time, or switching to a local donor whose seed does not involve shipment in a one-hundred-sixty-five-dollar tank. But we fear our children's father might live around the block, might be the creepy-looking man with the duffel bag we saw at the fertility center. And I have my thing about California donors being struggling artists and donors at other uncreative sites around the country being freaks. So California stays. Therapy goes. These are the first sacrifices. We are different already. We are so-o-o different now.

The IUI has not worked. I spot, cramp, and then bleed two days before my period is due. Monthly bleeding has not been this depressing since I was twelve and it happened for the first time, relegating me, or so I believed, to a life sans physical activity, sans running, jumping, skipping, swimming, or pretending I was a boy. It's over, I thought at age twelve. I'm a failure, I think at age thirty-nine. And all the years in between? Something along the continuum from inconvenience to surprise.

And this month my period means another six hundred dollars. A failed doctor-assisted attempt at pregnancy. Progesterone suppositories. A Cancer instead of a Gemini.

The thing about fertility centers is that their business is getting women pregnant. Numbers. So after one IUI and one home try it's intervention time. Not yoga or acupuncture or a weekend away but handmade progesterone tablets to be squeezed twice a day "Into, into…" the pharmacist stammers.

"My vagina."

"Yes, yes." He is so grateful for the assistance.

I order them and then change my mind. I decide to relax instead.

Perhaps it's a function of hope, of never believing I might not be pregnant that causes me to call my gynecologist and request a blood test despite having bled more or less on schedule. The thing is, my period was two days early and lasted only two days total. And all the books say you might still be pregnant even if you bleed a bit around the time or your period, so? Is it that ridiculous that here I sit waiting for a pregnancy blood test, fearing, of course, that I might have some dreadful disease? Any shrink would tell me, for a substantial sum, that the fear of having a dread disease that would render me infertile is a manifestation of my ambivalence about motherhood and pregnancy. A manifestation too of my incredible guilt or rage at my mother's reproductive cancer.

In *The Boston Globe* this morning there's a picture of women at a Ripley's Believe It or Not Museum in Myrtle Beach, S.C. They're standing in line to rub an African fertility goddess that looks exactly like the fertility goddess our friend gave us! The one who sits on the Crate and Barrel nightstand. The article says that rubbing the statue is supposed to enhance a woman's fertility. Rubbing her?! I'm so afraid even to brush against our goddess because she is so buxom and fertile and I have a kind of object crush on her (like having a crush on a house or a car) and I've been careful not to foist my perversion upon her. I'm careful not to place a hand on her for too long at a time. I even apologize to her when I have to move her. So, rub her?! Holy hell!

But it all makes sense. I'm afraid of my womanhood, afraid of desire, afraid of full breasts and thick thighs like tree trunks. I decide to conquer my fear and rub her. But where?

I start with her arms and shoulders, which seems benign enough.

"Rub her stomach," Faith suggests. "And her womb."

Okay, stomach, belly, protruding navel. A minute later I think I'm pregnant. Maybe I'm just aroused.

"Why don't you rub me like that?" Faith asks. and oy vey, we are faced with the fact that we have not had sex in a while, too long. And then we're on to that topic, which for long-term couples of any persuasion is the pit-of-hell topic. Because not having sex is like falling into a pit. At first you can see the light. At first you reach toward it and feel bad that it's so far away. But eventually you can't even see it, don't even look up for it, and instead you just curl up and fall asleep. Then you have to go to couples counseling and talk about the whole thing with a stranger who probably isn't having sex either but makes you feel freakish all the same, and that is the hell part.

I rub Faith's shoulders and arms and say, "It's just a phase." And then we curl back up in our pit and go to sleep.

Whoa. Margaret, our upstairs neighbor, has learned that her younger brother has been donating sperm to the same sperm bank from which she bought hers. The woman at the sperm bank insisted he tell Margaret after he casually mentioned one day on the phone that his older sister is in the process of getting pregnant via an anonymous donor. Margaret thinks she would have been able to detect her own family's history had she stumbled upon his profile—providing, of course, that her brother had been truthful about his number of siblings, medical history, etc. But I wonder.

I write down my own family's medical history as it would appear on a donor information sheet and am shocked to find that, given the option, I never would select myself as a donor, what with the assortment of cancer, alcoholism, and anxiety disorders that is sprinkled throughout my family like glitter at a preschool. Not only that, but I wouldn't even recognize myself if I came upon my own profile in a library of hundreds of others. How many of us identify with our medical and psychiatric histories?

It's good news, really. If I don't reflect all of the physical and psychological maladies of my medical history, then how much do we really need to worry about each and every infirmity of our chosen donor? Some of my best friends and most beloved neurotics would have truly scary donor profiles . So once again the ability to choose a medical history with which to mate (rather than the person attached to it) creates an overwhelming burden to make some unnaturally pure decision. The idea that medical histories, like SAT scores, are not accurate assessments of our personality and potential offers relief with regard to our "crazy decision," as we have come to term it.

I'm using two ovulation test kits at the same time, and according to one I'm having my LH surge but according to the other I'm not. I realize we've been putting all of our faith, money, and assumptions about my fertility into a kit that I purchased on sale for $15.99 at a drugstore. Despite the conflicting evidence regarding my current state of ovulation, we decide I should have the second IUI anyway.

It's even more uneventful than the first, if that's possible. Faith didn't even join me. I chatted during the procedure with the technician about HMOs and the state of health care. It was all I could do to remember not to go home and have a beer.

Two weeks later I get my period.

It dawns on us that our second IUI and third insemination has left us with only three more vials of semen. That means that even if I do happen to get pregnant the next time around there will only be two vials left for Faith to use when her turn comes. If I don't get pregnant I'll wind up using one or both of the remaining vials, and then there will be none left for Faith. Our plan to have biologically related children suddenly seems very tenuous. When we bought the initial six vials there was some sense that we were set for life—who would ever need more than six vials of semen? But we do. In particular, we need more of Baldie's semen. It is our first taste of how beyond our control the process of baby-making is. The six-vial plan, three for me and three for Faith, is bottoms up. You can't count on conceiving by a certain time. You can't decide to give birth during your summer vacation. You can't plan the physical and mental health of your child. You may not even be able to plan on there being a biological relationship between your child and that of your partner. You can't plan a thing.

But you can have incredibly good luck.

After I place my order for an IUI vial to be shipped in time for our next insemination, before I take a deep breath, cross my fingers, and venture to ask about the status of Baldie's total inventory, the woman tells me that another client who also had purchased a "mass quantity" of Baldie's sperm (ten vials) wants to sell it. Just like us, they had reserved a number of vials that were held in storage at the sperm bank until notification to ship them. And now they no longer want them.

"Why?" Faith mouths to me. "Ask them why they're selling it? W-H-Y?"

Despite the motility test run each month on our thawed specimens, Faith has begun to wonder whether there's something wrong with our donor. She heard some urban myth about a couple who couldn't get pregnant because the woman's healthy uterus had rejected the man's healthy sperm. Even though the couple loved each other very much, their genetic material just didn't get along.

Faith, in one of my ears, is reminding me of this story. "There's absolutely no scientific reason for it," she says. "They just reject each other." While in the other ear the woman at the sperm bank informs me that the couple has decided to adopt and are selling their vials because they need all the financial resources they can get their hands on.

"So they didn't get pregnant?"

"That's correct."

I ask the woman if anyone ever has become pregnant with Baldie's sperm. She pauses to consult a…list? A computer? The person watering her plants?

"No," she finally says.

"No," I mouth to Faith. She looks horrified.

The woman explains that Baldie hasn't been donating for very long and whenever a significant supply of his semen has accumulated, somebody—like us—buys it all. So in total, only three customers have attempted pregnancy with his sperm, including us. And that's just too few to determine there's a problem. Besides, each specimen is tested prior to freezing and then again after thawing at whatever site is doing the insemination.

By the way, there's one more thing we should know.

I can hardly wait. "What's that?"

"Your donor has stopped donating."

Jesus.

It's 4:45 in the afternoon, Pacific Standard Time. The sperm bank needs to know whether we would like to buy the ten vials, because if we don't, they will immediately try to sell them to another client. Of the ten vials, five are IUI and five are ICI. That's almost eighteen hundred dollars, not including shipping. And basically, it's our last chance.

We convince the sperm bank to give us until tomorrow at 9 A.M. Pacific Standard Time to let them know. Then we sit down at the kitchen table and try to figure out what the fuck to do.

Who could have anticipated the dilemma of having only two vials left? Having only two vials left is worse than having no vials left. Because when you have no vials left you and your partner are once again in the same boat: looking for a donor you both can use. But when you have only two vials left there's the possibility of getting pregnant without there being any sperm left over for your partner. It's like you always need six vials or five vials or four, but not two.

Meanwhile, do we really need twelve vials? There's this pressure to buy all ten because Baldie is gone (an otherwise positive piece of news, since our children will not have scores of other half siblings—in fact, they may not have any half siblings; we imagine he has struck it rich thanks to his incredibly smart genes and genetically good attitude and therefore no longer needs to sell his squirt for cash).

I pull out the calculator. Whenever I feel anxious and out of control I pull out the calculator and calculate and recalculate our finances. I can spend hours with the calculator. I think it is genetic, passed down to me from my father and grandfather—both accountants. This evening I spend three hours punching in actual numbers (what we have in our bank accountants) and then imaginary numbers (what we expect to have in our bank accounts in six months). I add and subtract and add again, squeezing and stretching anticipated overtime, money for a gig here, an article there. I punch in what we would have if we won $4,000 on a scratch card—no, $20,000, because Faith is usually the one to buy them and she would spend five dollars as opposed to my occasional one-dollar investment. It always comes to this. Bored and frustrated with our own finances, I start adding in fanciful winnings and optimal salaries. Until, yes, $200,000 tax-free is really the minimum amount it would take for us to feel financially comfortable.

By the end of the evening we decide on this: We'll purchase only those vials that are out of quarantine, i.e., ready to be shipped. That way we can save money by paying for only one nitrogen bomb tank instead of monthly ones. In addition, by having all of the vials shipped for storage in Boston we will spare ourselves two storage fees (Boston and L.A.).

According to the information given to us by the sperm bank woman a few hours ago, this means we'll be purchasing five more vials of sperm, giving us a total of seven.

In some ways it feels risky to have only seven vials. On the other hand, financially it's really all we can manage, if we want to someday clothe and shelter a child. One thousand forty dollars later we're back on track.

It's Halloween. A policeman just walked into the café in which I am stealing an hour, mumbling to himself, "Don't shoot until you see the whites of their eyes." I hope he's a crazy person dressed up in a policeman costume and not a crazy person who is a policeman.

Faith and I mailed the $1,040 check this morning before we left for work. We're feeling dangerously close to financial ruin in our quest to have a baby, and that seems horribly, bizarrely ironic. You're not supposed to have a child until you have enough money to support him or her. Yet in order to have this child we have to spend all the money we've saved in order to feel ready to have it. A child walks by the café window in a *Scream* costume. And then you have to be one of those parents who make their kids' Halloween costume, not some lazy depressed mother who sends her child out in a paper rendition of the terror of the moment. You must learn to accompany your child on his or her trick-or-treating expedition without being an overbearing embarrassment. You must carve pumpkins without instilling some form of knife phobia.

The Battles That Bond Us

(ROIDS, ROCK OPERAS, AND *MAD ABOUT YOU*)

As she fills my mother with chemotherapy, a nurse tells me about her fertility problems, how she needed shots and hormones and pills and was just about to give up ship when she and her husband decided to try "one more time." Voilà! They are now the proud parents of a beautiful baby girl. We are like two women chatting over coffee and a Danish, on a bus, at a health club, only it's the tenth-floor infusion room at the Dana-Farber Cancer Institute and my mother has cancer and is sitting next to us with a bag of Zofran slowly dripping into her through an I.V. My mother is smiling proudly, of course, because her daughter is all grown up and is talking with another woman about trying to have a baby. For seconds, maybe more, I forget why we are here. My mother tells the nurse about her upcoming trip to Los Angeles, about a sale at a local department store, the speed at which her dog chases pigeons at the park. The nurse smiles, replaces the I.V. tube with a test tube to draw a blood sample that will be analyzed for CA-125, the protein produced by ovarian cancer tumors and therefore a fairly reliable marker of the presence—or not—of the cancer. The nurse says she loves dogs and won't you have fun in Los Angeles. She puts the I.V. tube back in place so that my mother may receive the next ingredient in today's chemo cocktail, the steroid. The Zofran was for nausea. Before the Zofran were fluids. The steroid is administered to prevent my mother from having an allergic reaction to the star of the show, Gemcitabine. My mother loves this steroid. She claims it gives her tons of energy. The day after she gets it she cleans the house, gets out of bed at 3 A.M. to plan holiday presents for the family. She reminds me of this now, tells me she has a closet filled with gifts and not to snoop. The nurse tells us about a patient who, after receiving this same steroid, goes on a spending spree buying all sorts of unnecessary clothing that she returns two days later when the effect of the steroid wears off. We all laugh. My mother shows me a picture of a sweater she thinks I might like. The nurse agrees, it's perfect.

It's a beautiful sunny morning. My mother and I rarely get to spend a morning together. Dinner maybe. A late afternoon. But when since I have been living in my own house have I seen her in the morning? Only in Provincetown for one week of the year. I pour myself a cup of tea, get my mother a fruit cup from the snack cart. We are having such a good time. And then I remember why we are here and it is as if I am a cartoon character who, standing dumbly and innocently in space, happens to look down to find that she inadvertently has run over the edge of a cliff. And with that awareness it's, *Whoosh!* Down for the fall.

Aside from trying to get me pregnant and coping with her mother-in-law's battle with cancer, Faith is consumed by a rock opera she's writing, for which, in order to make back all of the money she has invested in production costs, she needs to sell seventeen hundred tickets. She is possessed. Spread out all over the dining room table, the kitchen table, and her desk, are lyric sheets, costume ideas, receipts, and hundreds of phone numbers. Eric, Faith's guitarist and musical director, returned from a sojourn in Spain with his girlfriend to live with us for two weeks. Faith is in her element. I am in hell.

We are due to inseminate in a few days and somebody is living with us, talking constantly about bar chords and card-stock mailers. Faith warned me. All the way back in September she sat me down and told me November was going to be hard because she'd be totally preoccupied with the rock opera and either we would be inseminating or I'd be pregnant and might feel that she's not involved enough. Eric might need to stay with us and things will be chaotic, so just try to understand.

"Sure," I said. "I support you and your work and the rock opera. If I'm not pregnant I'll probably want to try that month anyway, just to keep on track, even though there'll be a lot going on."

She said that was fine. And I said we'll get through it. Eric can stay. We'll be fine.

It's just that even when you're not pregnant and you're not inseminating, there's still a lot to talk about and a lot to decide, and Eric seems to interrupt us every time we have two minutes alone together. He's a nice guy and he cleans up after himself. But after the fifth night I think I might have to kill him.

I take walks and long baths and visit Simone in an effort to beat back my noncommunal nature. I tell myself time passes; nothing lasts forever. Eric wants to go back to Spain and his girlfriend, not live with us for the rest of his life. If Faith and I can't have a private conversation, well, at least we can sleep in the same bed at night. And look! One morning we even manage to detect my LH surge and arrange for insemination without Eric knowing.

We slip out the door early Sunday morning for my third IUI while Eric is still asleep. Unfortunately, after the procedure—which hurt like hell ("I hit a brick wall," the technician announced as she unsuccessfully tried to thread a catheter through my cervix and into my uterus)—Faith and I have a huge fight. It's cold and rainy, and because Eric is at the house we fight in the car. I am cramping and bleeding ("There is no brick wall," I wanted to tell the technician, "only my internal organs") and Faith is sobbing and blowing her nose into a sock because I don't have any Kleenex in the car. We're upset and angry and pathetic, parked against a curb around the block from our warm house.

I started it. Despite all of the preparation and warning, I told Faith that I felt she was disconnected and not supportive. I said I wanted to feel like this process, as well as our relationship, was precious and special. After the procedure I wanted her to put her arm around me and ask if she could take me to breakfast, rather than drag alongside me in rock opera–obsessed silence. One thing leads to another and soon we're discussing whether or not I pulled her into this, whether she is ready for parenthood, whether we are well-suited for each other. Seven and a half years and a mortgage later and maybe this all has been some terrible mistake. Maybe we're too different after all.

"So you never want to have children?" I ask, as, in my uterus, if we are lucky—or now, unlucky—sperm race like the wind with each other toward my unsuspecting egg.

"I do want to have children. I probably want to be pregnant more than you do."

How hard it must be to be the odd girl out of a lesbian couple, only one of whom gets pregnant at a time. If we were adopting a child, then our roles would be outwardly equal. If one of Faith's eggs were being injected into me she would be much more physically involved. Anything but this odd state of affairs in which we supposedly are having a biological child, when in actuality we're having my biological child. I ask her if this is what is going on, if she's mad at me, resentful, jealous.

"No."

Silly me.

"Besides, if you don't get pregnant and I try instead, I think I'd want a known donor."

Some issues between two adults are never, ever done. You learn after ten years or so that they never will be resolved, never will you reach agreement, never will one party say to the other, "Now I get it! You were right all along!" Instead the issues will follow you from year to year, place to place, like a skinny old cat or a plant that you've had since college that refuses to die, like your old futon or your high school yearbook, always there to remind you not to take anything for granted, never to lean back and fully relax.

And while most of these issues are present in some infinitesimal, minuscule, embryonic form on your first date, others, a select horrible few, emerge later in your relationship: the infidelity, the broken promise, the known donor.

"I thought we were done with that."
In response, Faith honks again into her sock.

Three days later I'm sick. Coughing until my throat bleeds, fever. It rains for five days straight and I'm sick for all of them. Eric leaves in disgust. Faith and I have another fight. This time about house guests and how she really wouldn't mind if someone stayed with us for a month, so how come I can only handle three days? And please, could I just hide it when I have reached the houseguest wall? Again, maybe we are too different, just too darned different to live together and have house guests.

Meanwhile, I pray that I'm not pregnant simply so that I may take pharmaceuticals other than Tylenol and Robitussin DM. I want codeine, ibuprofen, Valium. My fever reaches 101.2 degrees, and the fertility clinic goes into alert. If it hits 102 degrees, I'm to call my doctor immediately. I cough and take my temperature, cough and take my temperature, over and over again. I don't want to be pregnant. I don't want to spend nine months worrying about what this virus may or may not have done to our unborn child. I want my body back. I want Advil, and I want the rain to stop.

Tory delivers a challah and a new bottle of Robitussin. She informs me that Simone has stopped doing anything that she is told to do and when Tory and her boyfriend-coparent, Jay, get upset, instead of throwing a tantrum, Simone very calmly reasons with them. "I hear what you're saying, Mommy, but I'm still not ready to go." Tory and Jay envy other parents whose toddlers draw on the walls with red crayons or throw over lamps in the living room. It's all so simple: acting out and discipline, acting out and discipline. I remember months ago baby-sitting Simone and her convincing me she was allowed to go to bed with a bottle by gently patting my arm and saying, "It's okay, Harlie, don't worry." I tell her mother it's obvious she is either a psychopath or a lawyer.

I can't begin to imagine what I would do with a child who refused to listen to me, who figured out early on like my mother's Cairn terrier, that no matter the transgression, I always will feed and shelter and love him or her. So, why listen? If he or she is smart enough, it seems entirely possible to have a child without remorse.

It doesn't help that I am working on a research project now looking at schizophrenia as the possible result of some prenatal virus. I imagine my own little budding psychopath, disturbed beyond belief thanks to this flu. I can see the doctors and lawyers and police officers pointing at me in a courthouse and sadly shaking their heads, "If it wasn't for that virus she contracted three days after insemination her little one would be a concert pianist today and not facing fifteen to life." I continue wishing that I'm not pregnant this round. But that would mean another failed IUI. And then what?

My father calls to see how I'm feeling and to find out whether I'm pregnant. One thing leads to another, and within minutes we are engaged in our current favorite topic of conversation, his girlfriend's daughter-in-law, Allison.

My father, a conservative and practical corporate accountant who spends Sundays dressed in neat pleated slacks and a button-down Brooks Brothers shirt, has a much more matter-of-fact approach to life and money than me, his oldest daughter: At age twenty-two you graduate from college, get a job, and immediately make enough money to support yourself and eventually buy a house.

When I graduated from college with a bachelor's degree in sociology and no idea whatsoever how to make a living because the only things I knew how to do were write and paint and have late-night philosophical discussions about life and eternity, my father was caught off-guard. "But you went to Brandeis," he said.

"Allison," my father tells me now, "has really got a good thing going."

Allison brokers office supplies. She knows where to get things really cheap and where to sell them for more money. She does this all over the phone. Never touches the stuff she buys and sells, has no warehouse or anything. She doesn't program in Java or make Web pages, just sits on the phone all day buying and selling desks and computers and file folders.

"She's making $200,000 a year," my father tells me.

I try to imagine how someone thinks of such a thing to do, how they know the places to buy things cheap and then the places to sell them.

"Why don't the buyers just go directly to the first place?"

"No," my father says, exasperated. It's almost twenty years later, and still he's trying to get the same point across. And still I have no idea what it is. "She brokers the deal."

Simultaneously I think that I wish I had thought of such a thing and that it sounds so incredibly boring that if I had, I might also have to kill myself. I think that I will be doomed forever to a life of financial struggle because I can't get excited about things that involve computers or computer parts or toner cartridges or making money.

A week before this installment of our ongoing Allison conversation, my father sent Faith and me $1,000 to assist in our journey to parenthood. And while that was a hugely generous and supportive gesture, I feel certain he would be prouder of me if I were brokering office supplies by phone and not working in academia, hustling short stories, and living with a musician. Maybe parents just don't want to worry about their children. Face it, having a gay artist for a daughter is cause for much concern.

"Would you like to go into business with me selling stuff?"

He chuckles nervously.

I tell him not to worry, that I'm going to become hugely rich one day from writing short fiction. This time he laughs out loud. Then his girlfriend of ten years, an independently wealthy attorney, gets on the phone to tell me that Ms. Computer Parts will be joining us for Thanksgiving.

"I told her you're interested in learning about her business," his girlfriend, Linda, tells me.

The whole idea triggers a coughing fit and I accidentally hang up on her. I call back to explain, but still it seems they both have taken it personally.

Faith and I have not shared a bed in five days, since I started coughing. She is sleeping in the TV room, with the TV, of course, and her computer and a queen-size futon all to herself. I am in the bedroom with a humidifier, Kleenex, Robitussin, and the antibiotic I was told to take so that whatever has taken over my body does not turn into pneumonia. I am reading *Angela's Ashes* and have our bed all to myself to cough and sneeze and sweat in till the cows come. In the morning I ask Faith how she slept and she responds, "Perfect."

Ordinarily this kind of thing might cause me to worry that Faith wants to break up and sleep apart forever. But thanks to an episode of *Mad About You,* I know that we are completely normal. In that episode Jamie and Paul somehow get into the habit of sleeping in separate rooms, she in the bedroom with the telephone and he on the sofa with a beer. Friends come by, see the blankets on the sofa, and ask who's visiting. When Jamie and Paul confess that no one is staying over, everyone worries that their relationship is on the rocks. So many people are worried about them and the state of their union that they start to worry too. Twenty minutes later, not including commercials, Jamie and Paul realize there is nothing wrong with them, thank you very much, and this realization causes them to miss each other so much that they start sleeping in the same bed again. Anyway, if it weren't for this television sitcom I might worry that now my relationship with Faith is in trouble, what with our recent fighting and Faith sleeping on the futon, but thanks to prime time I know we're totally normal. If I still was in therapy, I would have to discuss all of this ad nauseam, but I'm getting pregnant instead, saving money, and therefore must rely on television for all in-depth personal analysis. It all makes me feel so normal, so mainstream, so much a part of the world. No longer am I a childless thirty-nine-year-old in therapy to dwell on my same-sex relationship. I am trying to get pregnant. I am prime time. I am the Buchmans.

Infertility?

(MORE CANCER AND A PAIR OF PLEATHER PANTS)

My mother takes a break from chemotherapy and flies to California to spend Thanksgiving with my sister, Carrie, and her husband, Kevin. Faith and I travel to Connecticut to ring in Thanksgiving with my father and his girlfriend. We are scheduled to leave Thanksgiving morning at 9:30 A.M. At 8 A.M. I get my period. I learn later my sister is menstruating too, and then Faith gets hers the next day. It's like red tide, like some bloody feminist revolution.

Aside from relief (the fever, the antibiotic, the four hundred milligrams of ibuprofen, the gallons of Robitussin DM—all would have caused me to worry over the neurological health of our child at least until he or she turned twenty-two and graduated from college), aside from the thrill of being able to gobble ibuprofen and Sudafed to my heart's content, aside from all the mixed feelings is this: I have a problem. Three IUI's and still I'm not pregnant. We schedule a consultation with a fertility doctor who tells us my HMO will cover the cost of the consultation and all future IUI's because after three doctor-assisted tries I'm now considered infertile.

When I think about that—my potential, unexpected infertility—I think about my huge, overwhelming ambivalence regarding parenthood and feel certain that it's this that is in the way. As if some tangible, possibly biochemical, xenophobic manifestation of my fear is holding up a sign that says GO AWAY! to the innocent sperm deposited in my uterus like immigrants dropped off at Ellis Island. As if my ambivalence is layering brick walls around my ovaries, putting up razor wire and electric fences, escorting my monthly ovum in handcuffs down the shoot and *Out! Out! Out!* of my body.

But then, haven't we paid our dues? Hasn't selecting a sperm donor, paying for semen, and not being able to hold hands in public earned Faith and me immunity from infertility? Isn't there some sort of obstacles quota?

I'm not sure how far I would go. Would I inject myself with hormones, risk a multiple birth, have eggs harvested from my body like cranberries from a bog? If this were about blending my genes with Faith's, I know I'd feel more motivated. I'd be driven by the sheer extraordinariness of joining our physical essences, by the unalienable right of sexual partners to merge their identities into a whole new human being. But the mixing of my genetics with that of a stranger is a much more tenable goal, much more precarious a mountain for my ambivalence and suspicion of all things medical to scale.

Perhaps the trade-off for not being able to procreate with my partner is the blessing of a spare womb. We don't have to enlist all of the various high-tech fertility tools at our disposal to have a biological child. Faith could try. If

I'm willing to forgo the experience of carrying a child, I can still participate in birth and parenting.

Aside from red tide, another epidemic follows us to my father's house: cancer. His girlfriend, Linda, is fighting the good fight with metastasized lung cancer. At one point my mother and Linda were receiving the exact same chemotherapy cocktail. My sister and I don't think it's unreasonable, therefore, to wonder whether our father causes cancer, whether there is something toxic about his anatomy, or his hormones, or the way he manages money. And while any Freudian worth his or her Oedipal salt would have a field day with all of this, it seems our father has started to wonder too. For a period of a few months, around the time when my mother had her first recurrence and Linda her initial diagnosis, my father walked around looking all guilty and omnipotent. I could tell he felt awful and somehow responsible for the diagnoses of the only two women he has been romantically committed to in his life. It wasn't until my sister rudely suggested, "Maybe it's you," that he snapped out of it. Sometimes you just need someone to put your worst fear out there so you can say out loud, "Oh, give me a break!" in an angry way and move on. This is why when the HMO refers to me as infertile, part of me wilts and another pronounces, "Oh, give me a break. It's only been three times."

Anyway, there's no way for Faith and me to have a Thanksgiving free of cancer and sorrow and the ravages of chemotherapy, and I can't help but wonder if all of that may have just a little bit to do with the status of my fertility.

The computer parts broker is at Thanksgiving in Connecticut and she's wearing *pleather* pants and a big diamond ring and all I can think whenever she walks into the room is, *She's rich, she's rich, she's rich. She brokers computer parts, and I don't.* I try to avoid her so I can avoid myself and my feelings of financial inadequacy, but she wants to talk to us about fertility because she knows what we're up to (who doesn't) and she herself had to do the whole hormone-shot thing.

Allison can't say enough about progesterone. Progesterone! Progesterone! Progesterone! She thinks it gets your body ready, wakes your reproductive system up from its deep, childless slumber, gets everything all moist and warm and receptive. Her husband, Linda's oldest son, interrupts her to offer us sperm. It's a joke, putting one arm around me and the other around Faith, a real knee-slapper. We laugh, ha ha ha. Wouldn't that be weird? Ha ha. He has red-wine breath and an overhanging gut that in another day and age would induce visions of opulence, but in the year 2000 is just plain icky. I think of our sperm donor, our bald struggling writer who loves to cook, and I wish he were here. I'm certain he wouldn't have red-wine breath and be thrusting his genes all around the room. I want to tell Allison, the rich computer parts broker, "You didn't have to marry him. Look at you! You could have bought as much sperm as you wanted".

Today's cover story in *The Boston Globe*'s Living section is about sperm donation! It's all about the coming of age of the first generation of children conceived by anonymous sperm donors. The author covers everything from donor profiles to yes donors to the cost of a vial of semen. She discusses what it may be like when children meet their anonymous fathers and half-siblings. She mentions the picture bank. She interviews past and present donors, adolescent and adult children of anonymous artificial insemination. But not once—not once!—does she mention lesbians. There is not one single reference to the very reason her topic is so hot in the first place: More women are buying sperm because gay women are buying sperm. It's November 2000 and this is Boston and not once does the author mention homosexuality in her entire two-page article about sperm donation!

I want to write a letter to the *Globe,* but I'm tired of writing angry letters to the *Globe,* which offends me every other week. I'm afraid of becoming my ninety-two-year-old Uncle Freddie, who writes every day to the New Jersey *Star Ledger* on behalf of senior citizens. Instead I mop the floors with Murphy's Oil Soap, water the plants, and go on strike by refusing to read the paper for three days or until I need to see a movie schedule, whichever comes first.

The Month Off

(DR. $ AND THE DEAD OF WINTER)

We are interim, taking the much-touted month off from trying to get pregnant. It feels like getting off a carnival ride, like sitting down with cotton candy to watch as everyone else continues to dip and dive, rock and swirl without you. If only you hadn't gotten so nauseous!

It's December 2000, and the air is starting to bite my bare skin with little razor-sharp teeth. The word "barren" pops into my mind more often than I would like. As in, there is not a leaf in sight upon the barren winter landscape. As in, she is childless, that barren thirty-nine-year-old woman. There is no president-elect. We have enough sperm for the next seven months, and I am technically infertile so we no longer have to shell out $615 per month in baby-making fees. It all adds up to one thing: It's time to return to therapy.

My therapist, a heterosexual woman in her mid fifties, believes it doesn't matter at all (!) that she's straight and I'm gay. In fact, she's so supportive of my sexual orientation that I've become convinced over the years that treatment with me has brought her to the brink of homosexuality, that a few more sessions together and she might ditch her husband and rush sweating and trembling into the arms of some red-hot little mama. However, since she all too gleefully would attribute this theory to transference, I refuse to share it with her.

We make an appointment to reunite in two weeks. I think she sounds delighted. But that too is probably just transference rearing its horny little head.

In the meantime I distract myself from myself by reading Jon Krakauer's *Into Thin Air*. So that every night before I fall asleep, rather than ruminate over infertility, finances, and whether to enroll our future children in the Boston public school system, I thank my lucky stars I'm not climbing Mount Everest in a blizzard. And then the bed feels warmer, the oxygen-laden air sweeter, our one bathroom a luxury of Sotheby's proportion.

Two nights before our appointment with the fertility doctor I dream I'm going to be inseminated in front of sixteen friends for whom I first have to make lasagna. Once everyone has their food I am led away by a nurse.

My mother and I are swimming side by side again. Tomorrow, while Faith and I are at the fertility clinic, it turns out my mother will be at the Dana-Farber Cancer Institute finding out the results of a recent PET scan. The decision to attend our appointment rather than accompany my mother ripped my heart and stomach out of my body and placed them back in again upside-down and broken. It was my mother who insisted we keep our appointment.

"Go find out about that grandchild."

My mother and I told each other that if her visit involved pain, physical pain, I'd be there. If she were feeling sick or if she hadn't just had a relatively reassuring CT scan, I would be there, if the sky were gray instead of blue, if it were Monday instead of Friday. All along, since my mother's diagnosis four and a half years ago, we've told ourselves a whole variety of relative and ridiculous things to justify the continuation of our own lives and grant ourselves some illusion of relief. We tell each other that even though the cancer is proving to be somewhat treatment-resistant, at least it's not spreading. Then, even though it's spreading, at least it's not spreading fast or to places that are hard to reach surgically. We tell ourselves that the fact that our mother has survived almost five years since her diagnosis means she will beat this thing, even though only two and a half of those years have been spent in blessed remission. My mother tells my sister and me these relative joys so that we'll go on with life as usual and not worry so much. My sister and I tell each other these things so that she won't want to hang herself for living all the way in Los Angeles, and so that I will not curl up in a helpless ball here in Boston.

Now we tell ourselves Friday will be fine! Normal, like it is for other normal people. Mom will go to the doctor to find out if the cancer has spread, and Harlie and Faith will go to the doctor and find out why Harlie isn't getting pregnant. Later we'll call each other up and share the news!

It's the morning of cancer/fertility Friday. A sheet of ice covers our porch and the sidewalk. I say a prayer for my mother, for her body and spirit, for the cancer to be gone or at least subdued. I throw in a quick plug for my own uterus and ovaries. Faith tells me she'll do the same, and by the way, "Don't worry, I'll dress appropriately for the doctor."

"Thank you."

It's awful to imagine one spouse telling another how to dress. Reprehensible. To think someone would ever tell their thirty-six-year-old lover that torn cords, a T-shirt, and a gangsta-style ski hat embarrass her, especially when visiting the same fertility clinic that required them to see a social worker—it's sad, really. Wouldn't that indicate all sorts of inappropriate parent-child aspects of the relationship? Wouldn't that imply that the couple was hanging together by a mere thread?

"I'll wear a dress," Faith tells me.

Cute.

"And lipstick."

"See you at 1:30."

"Don't forget to douche."

Fuck off.

The cancer has not spread. We are so relieved. However, chemo has been canceled until further notice because, while the cancer did not spread, it did not shrink or go away either, and there's no use in continuing to poison my mother if the poison isn't doing any good. But we're so relieved that we hardly care about that. It's not spreading! It's not spreading! My mother and I discuss where to get the best kosher turkey, whether or not to make a BJ's run this weekend. We grab hold of any silver lining and soar with it into the night.

And then Faith and I visit the fertility clinic, and the day deteriorates. The fertility doctor, a woman I will refer to as

Dr. $, greets us with a huge smiling hello and two firm handshakes. A female medical resident with the bedside manner of a bull mastiff sits in the chair to Dr. $'s left, where she seems to be expending a great deal of mental energy avoiding eye contact with either Faith or me.

Once Dr. $'s smile fades it's clear she has no idea why we are there.

"Well, I've had three failed IUI's and I thought it might be time to check in. I wondered if a lot of women require more than three IUI's to get pregnant or if it was time to see if something is wrong."

Dr. $ glances down at my chart, closes it, and announces it's time for injections. She reminds me that I am thirty-nine years old and there is no time to waste, so let's introduce injectable hormones, whose role it will be to stimulate my ovaries to produce eggs. As in more than one. As in multiple births.

Wait a minute. Don't we need to find out if anything is wrong with me? Whether I even need more eggs? Aren't there several steps in between what we're doing and injections? Maybe what we need is more sperm. Most of the women I know who've gotten pregnant via an intrauterine insemination of thawed donor sperm have had two IUI's each cycle. Frozen sperm lives only twenty-four hours in the uterus as compared to the relatively long 120-hour life span of fresh sperm (i.e., your husband or boyfriend or KD1 or KD2). So maybe if I've been just six or twelve hours off in calculating my ovulation, then the sperm is dying too soon. Or maybe I should have an ultrasound to see if I have a uterine polyp.

"Maybe we first should find out what's wrong with me. Maybe I have a uterine polyp."

"Why would you have a polyp?"

"Well, because I did have a polyp. Remember, you saw it on an ultrasound and suggested I have it removed as it was likely to make it difficult to maintain a pregnancy?"

REMEMBER?!

"And that was in February?"

"No, April."

"So it's gone."

"Yes, but you told me it could come back within a year. So I just wondered if that was something we might want to check."

YOU INSENSITIVE SHIT!

"I don't see any reason to do an ultrasound. And I don't see any reason to waste time with Clomid [an oral ovulation stimulant], as nothing but injections will ultimately be more effective than what you've been doing, natural IUI's."

"And the progesterone suppositories?"

"You don't need progesterone suppositories because your progesterone levels are fine."

AND HOW DO WE KNOW THEY ARE FINE? BECAUSE EVEN THOUGH YOU PRESCRIBED THE SUPPOSITORIES WITHOUT TESTING ME FIRST, I INSISTED ON HAVING A BLOOD TEST TO SEE IF I REALLY NEEDED THEM. AND APPARENTLY I DIDN'T! SO WHY WOULD I BELIEVE YOU NOW, YOU CORPORATE WHORE?

"Of course," she steals a glance at Faith, who, although she is wearing jeans without holes and a nice shirt, has forgotten to brush her hair, "injection cycles are very expensive. So if your insurance company is not willing to pay, you might want to discuss how realistic that procedure is for you."

FUCKING JUDGMENTAL CLASSIST HOMOPHOBE!

"We *have* budgeted for *all* of this," I tell her, even though we haven't.

"And you might want to begin thinking about what you would do should you have a multiple birth."

Does she talk like this to all her clients? Does she jump the gun and presume financial incompetence with the women whose husbands are sitting beside them in a suit and tie? With the lesbians in pantsuits and makeup? Does she immediately dose all of her patients with potent synthetic hormones regardless of their family histories and medical status? I just want to know. I'm just CURIOUS, THAT'S ALL.

The next day I feel sick, beaten up, run over by a medical Mack truck. I'm worried about my mother, who is now scheduled for an infusion of chemotherapy directly into the resistant cancerous lesions that have set up shop in her liver—a dangerous and debilitating procedure we had hoped to avoid. I'm worried about myself. I feel dangerously close to old age. I feel eighty, ninety, 101, hunched over and toothless. Yet despite our dream of attaining a "geriatric pregnancy," neither Faith nor I believe it is time for hormonal injections. We tell ourselves they're just trying to boost their statistics. We're part of the machine, the fertility assembly line.

And what about all of the steps Dr. $ so cavalierly dismissed: blood tests to more accurately monitor ovulation, an ultrasound to make sure my physiology is A-okay, an additional IUI each cycle? Not to mention that injectable fertility drugs have been suspected of increasing a woman's risk of developing ovarian cancer.

On our way out the door I had said to Dr. $, "So, you think continuing with a few more natural IUI's is a waste of time?"

Her answer: "No, not at all."

We decide to get another opinion. In the meantime, we'll continue at least one more cycle sans intervention, just to see what happens. IUI round four is two and a half weeks away, directly between Christmas and New Year's. To boost our chances we spend $45 on a super-duper ovulation predictor kit. For good measure, I make an appointment with Martha the needle-hair Japanese acupuncturist and schedule a tune-up.

Families American-Style

(THE PSYCHOANALYST AND THE LESBIAN)

Rain, lightning, thunder. The wind is like an angry toddler, stirring everything up to get our attention, pushing our hair into our eyes and pulling the hats from our heads, just because. We are five days from Hanukkah, eight days from Christmas, and it is a bizarre and stormy sixty degrees along the Northeast coast. My mother remarks how grateful she is to have hair and not a wig on a day like this. "It would blow right off," she says. I take a deep breath. She's about to lose it again, her hair. I wonder if she knows. I think she knows but isn't talking about it. I don't say anything because I'm sure she knows. Why press the point? She just doesn't want to mention it, doesn't want to imagine the horror of the preparatory haircut, the first few weeks of hair loss. So, "Yeah," I say. "Good thing."

Over the phone, Boston to Los Angeles and back again, my sister and I go into battle mode, planning shifts for our mother's upcoming hepatic infusion. Carrie will come in for a week, and then I will cover the rest. One week for her, fifty-one for me. I try not to feel resentful because it is our mother after all and we love her and imagine how horrible it would be if she weren't here to worry about and to take care of. That's the alternative now, her not being here, and I'm all the time weighing it against the responsibility and worry and obligation. Imagine, I tell myself, if she were gone. Still, despite my tears, I sometimes get all twisted out of shape about the part-time versus full-time status that differentiates my sister's role from my own. To make matters more complex and competitive, Carrie ended our last conversation with, "I stopped taking the pill."

Fine. She lives what seems like a perpetual L.A. vacation, sailing while we shovel snow, hiking the canyons in shorts and a T-shirt while we apply extra-strength moisturizer to our cracked skin. She got the wedding, the presents, the showers, the bicoastal engagement parties, my estranged parents to come together for a familial stroll down the aisle, and now, to top it off, she has her very own sperm bank complete with fresh free-range sperm guaranteed to live for 120 hours in the privacy of her undisturbed womb.

"I don't think we'll tell people when we're trying," she whispers into the phone.

You just did.

That night I dream my sister is using a blow dryer in the bathtub. "Stop!" I scream. "You'll electrocute yourself!" Fifteen years and seven million dollars worth of therapy just so that my hostility may be masked as a heroic deed.

Here's how my parents' marriage ended: One day, years after my parents finally had stopped fighting and bickering all the time, my father fell in love with another woman. I was twenty-nine years old and Carrie twenty-six when my mother gave us the news.

"The fucker's got a girlfriend."

A girlfriend? Our father, who was so shy he had difficulty talking with his own family, went out and met a woman? We couldn't imagine it. Aside from our feelings about the betrayal and the pain he had caused our mother, we just couldn't picture him lusting after someone, going out and having a conversation, dating.

Unfortunately, something about the occasion of his having fallen in love with another woman also caused our father to make some terrible financial decisions. So that by my 30th birthday my upper-middle-class Jewish parents not only were separated but also had dropped several notches down the federal withholding ladder. It was a very bad year. But we've had worse, like the year my grandmother suffered a cerebral hemorrhage the same month my mother was diagnosed with cancer.

Anyway.

This all to say that my potential infertility is not huge and scary or even particularly depressing. It's just annoying. Just one more fucking thing. But it's not life or death. It's not pain and suffering. It's not watching your fifty-six-year-old mother move from the family house into a small apartment because there are liens on her savings accounts, not like cancer, or bringing your grandmother by ambulance from New Jersey to a nursing home in Boston, where she will spend the rest of her life. Infertility is surmountable. It comes with options and alternatives, and at the end of the day you still get to go home and sleep in your very own bed and wake up and have a cup of tea.

In the grand scheme of things, I simply feel aggravated.

Pissed. I want to tell somebody off. But I don't feel like crying. At least not yet.

After a two-and-a-half-month hiatus, my therapist and I reunite long enough for her to explain to me that, in her opinion, Dr. $ recommended injections because time is of the essence, not because she thought—or even cared—that something is wrong. The only problem, apparently, is that I'm thirty-nine years old and there isn't a lot of time to waste. I suppose when you're twenty-six you can screw around all you want with natural IUI's and relaxation techniques.

What do you know.

We discuss my ambivalence over and over again. "Why?" my therapist wants to know. Why am I so ambivalent? Why do I doubt my ability to raise a child? What is it that I think I don't have that everybody else has?

A husband?

More money?

A husband?

It always boils down to this: Maybe I don't deserve to have a stable life and family because I'm gay. Maybe there is something wrong with me. Maybe, as Freud suggested, I am fixated at some premature developmental stage and therefore not capable of conquering what the rest of the world conquers. Maybe I have no right to impose this freakish stunted growth of mine on another living being. And despite their support, I know I've disappointed my parents on some deep evolutionary level, and for that maybe I don't deserve to have my own family.

My therapist gives me a look that conveys the "Give me a fucking break" she is not allowed to say. She wants me to get to it, the true source of my deep-seated fear of managing in an adult world. And sexual orientation is just not it. Apparently, there are other far more interesting reasons for my fears of loving a child too much or not enough, for being afraid that I'm too selfish and anxious and deeply sad a person to be a mother. Apparently, in comparison to everything else in my life—family, friends, art, the tulips growing in the backyard, the great Goshawk outside my window at work—the fact of my being gay is relatively boring.

Each week I secretly scan the other patients in the waiting room: the graying man who intentionally eyeballs me on his way out the door and leaves the office reeking of cigarette smoke, the sad-eyed woman with full makeup and hair dyed an odd blend of copper and magenta who mournfully goes in after me. Do they really know something I don't know? Are they really better suited to be parents simply because of the number of orifices their sexual partners have?

At home, Faith is baking a chicken and transcribing music. The kitty is fast asleep on our bed. The plants all seem to be thriving. Nothing about our life together resembles developmental apocalypse. Perhaps I do use my sexual orientation as an excuse for avoiding insecurities far more complex and interesting. Perhaps we're just fine, no more confused and neurotic than the general population. Maybe, just maybe, a child would be very lucky to live here with the two of us.

Revelations

(WHITE-COLLAR CRIME AND THE ROAD TO
WELLVILLE)

At her request I am stealing Carrie a Hanukkah present
from the hospital where I work: pregnancy tests. I find two
cartons in the lab; one contains tests that will expire in May
2001, the other, tests that will expire in August 2002. I grab
eight (her lucky number) from the August carton—no sense
in rushing her—and shove them into my bag.

The only guilt I experience has to do with the wish
that my sister not get pregnant before me. As for the
white-collar crime, I am sadly without remorse. Faith was
right: It's *my* genetic material we need to worry about,
not some donor's.

In a dream I look down and in my hand are all of our stored
vials, perfectly thawed even though it's three days before I'm
due to ovulate! Each vial is warm—no, hot. Too hot. Have I
destroyed a $1,000 worth of semen? And why did I thaw all of
them when I wasn't even ovulating? Can you refreeze semen,

use some, and then put it back in the freezer for next week like eggplant parmesan or chicken cacciatore?

Faith is in L.A. for Christmas to watch her nephew open presents, soak up the sunshine, and wander around Echo Park and Silver Lake with her sister.

Alone for a week in Boston, I do what I love to do when Faith is gone: clean incessantly. It takes three days for me to clean the entire house. It's part of some kind of get-back-to-myself ritual, so that by the fourth day I'm whole and in my element. I start with the bathroom because it's disgusting, Shit Beach having spread beyond the litter box and frighteningly close to the bathtub. I scrub the tub and the tile wall, and then I mop the floor, change the litter, and vacuum the cruddy little rug the box sits on. With surgical gloves (also swiped from the hospital) protecting me from the poisons of cleanliness I clean the toilet bowl inside and out. With the bathroom finished, I'm about to move on to the next room when for some reason it occurs to me that I should meditate. I haven't meditated in close to eight years, since Faith and I got together, but apparently all of that's going to change because I'm pulling my meditation cushion out from a closet and removing my shoes.

Before I attempt to stop my thoughts for twenty endless minutes, I think a whole lot about everything, including meditation. I resolve to meditate once a day, and that will be good. Better than hormone injections. It will help me handle the baby-making process, my relationship with Faith, my mother's illness. For twenty minutes a day I will still the perpetual motion that is my body and mind.

It is eighteen degrees outside and inside I'm warm and dry, free to decide to meditate or cook or clean, make a phone call or take a bath. If we have a baby it will never be like this again. Even children grown and far away are with you always. Being ready to have a baby is being ready to give this up. I wonder: Am I ready for this to be the last time I have absolute privacy, quiet, space, self-centeredness? Have I had enough freedom to open myself to responsibility, obligation, somebody else's life?

Maybe it's something about the air, or maybe it's having had a whole week in which to gorge myself on privacy that causes me finally to feel full, sated, to think, *Okay, I've had my share.* The house is clean. I have had my own room, gotten into graduate school, dropped out of graduate school. I have fallen in love, out of love, then back in love again. I have lived alone, learned to drive a stick shift, bake bread, and climb a mountain. It's time for the next thing. I'm ready. And because I'm thinking about meditation, about mind versus body and how interconnected but perhaps ultimately separate each can be, I think, *Well, then I must inform my body.* If I'm ready then I must let my body know. In some sense my body has been protecting my spirit, warding off invasion because, despite all that I've said and done, I have not been ready at all.

I tell my body, "Okay. I am ready now. I can let go of this era. I can open my heart and take care of somebody else. It's okay to get pregnant."

And then I sit.

I call the fertility clinic and schedule a double, a one-two punch: two consecutive IUI's. The first will take place the day of my LH surge, the second the following day. All along the fertility clinic has been suggesting that two IUI's are unnecessary. But everyone we know who has gotten pregnant—quickly—with frozen donor sperm has had two consecutive

IUI's. We're propelled both by our lack of faith in the motives of the fertility clinic as well as by that daunting equation: Frozen sperm lives for twenty-four hours, ovulation can occur from twelve to thirty-six hours after your LH surge, the onset of which, as we know, is being predicted by a store bought kit. What if I test myself at noon but my surge really began the night before? What if the kit is bad? It makes sense to pull out all the guns, to shoot from both hips, to bring in the tanks. *Bang! Bang!*

For three afternoons in a row two rainbows have appeared on the windowsill in my kitchen. They must be cast by the crystal from my grandmother's chandelier in the dining room, or from the small square of stained glass in the window. They are two perfectly round rainbows, more like rainbow blobs or rainbow amoebas than rainbows as in "Somewhere over the Rainbow." I tell myself they are evidence I will soon be pregnant, each rainbow being a spirit come to greet me. This means, in my rainbow logic, that if I do get pregnant I likely will have twins. On the fourth day one rainbow merges with the other, and I am so relieved.

Faith returns from Los Angeles at midnight on December 28. At 10:30 the following morning we're squinting at the two pink lines of our super-duper ovulation tester to determine whether the pink test line indeed is darker than the pink reference line. It would be easier to detect bacteria on our countertop, the gender of a newborn kitten. I can say with certainty that the test line is darker than it was the day before. Yesterday, when Faith was bidding her nephew a tearful farewell, there was practically no test line. Just a reference line. Today, with Faith back home and jet-lagged, her suitcase still somewhere in Detroit or Los Angeles or London, the test line is definitely visible. But is it darker than the reference line? We stare and stare and then close our eyes and stare some more.

"Uh-oh." Faith reads the instructions. "Do not read the test after five minutes!"

As if we might go blind. As if deciphering shades of pink is akin to taking in a solar eclipse with the naked eye rather than with a piece of cardboard with a hole in it. Be careful, you people intent on breeding even though the world already is populated enough! Be careful not to burn your retinas!

Of course it's just that the test line either fades or becomes deceivingly dark after five minutes. Of course. I don't need my therapist to tell me that one.

Also stated in the instruction manual is this: "If the test line is darker than or as dark as the reference line then you're surging."

The nurse at the fertility clinic wishes us a happy New Year and schedules an appointment for us for tomorrow.

"We wanted to come in today too."

She reminds us that really isn't necessary, that in their opinion two IUI's are no better than one.

"We feel more comfortable trying twice." We have told ourselves that if I am not pregnant in two months we will find another doctor, but for the sake of convenience we will continue to have natural IUI's performed at our current, potentially malevolent, fertility clinic. Baldie is stored there. The second-floor lab responsible for thawing him and testing his motility is considered one of the best in town. As long as we know what we want and what we don't want, we think we can manage.

"All right," is her reluctant answer.

IUI A is scheduled for 1 o'clock this afternoon. Assuming we leave the house by 12:20, that gives us three hours to wait for the suitcase to arrive from its vacation in Detroit. IUI B is 10 o'clock tomorrow morning, two hours before we're due to be hit with the first blizzard of the season.

Isn't It Romantic Double-Take

("S" My Name Is Sarah)

12:20 P.M. I'm sitting alone in the car with my hand on the horn trying to not to blow it. Faith is inside the house getting her coat, finding a pair of gloves, writing a note to the airline people should they happen by with her luggage while we are away. Our planned departure time is now, 12:20, but I'm calm and serene thanks to having meditated seven days in a row, so my hand is on the horn but I'm not yet pressing down on it.

12:21 P.M. It must be Faith's tremendous ambivalence that's causing her to be so incredibly late and passive-aggressive. I almost press down on the horn but weigh the effect of that gesture against the fact that we really are just talking about a minute. One minute! Because I'm so serene I smile to myself and turn on the radio.

12:22 P.M. I am losing all faith in our ability to raise children together and have a relationship. I should leave without her. It is her problem, her ambivalence, her demons, and I, being so calm, should simply leave without her. I press just a bit on the horn to see what happens. If sound comes out, so be it. If not then I am still coming across as cool, calm, and collected. I glance up and see a white sheet of paper being slapped against the storm door. The airline note. Okay, at last. I am so glad I didn't beep the horn. After all, we're only talking about two minutes!

12:23 P.M. It's been like a fucking hour since the note to the airline people was taped to the door and still no Faith. What the hell is she doing? Ruining my chances of becoming a parent? Imposing her ambivalence on me? If she's so ambivalent she doesn't have to come, does not even have to be involved with me. She can leave and I will raise a baby on my own. I can buy out her half of the house and move in with my mother. I cannot believe we are back to square one on the weekend of our double-whammy.

Beep!

Faith waves at me through the window.

12:24 P.M. We are in the car and on our way.

"I had to write a note to the airline people."

At least I don't stay mad. At least we don't mention the horn or have a fight. While as impatient as ever, at least I'm learning to let things go, getting mad and moving on. Besides, the gas tank reads empty and the fuel light is coming on. I may be compulsively on time, but I hurl far bigger obstacles across our path. There is exactly thirty-five cents in my wallet and no gas in the car. Faith shakes her head and leans back. She is so much kinder than I.

After riding on fumes to the nearest gas station, we arrive at the fertility clinic to find the waiting area entirely empty. It's a strange relief, like finding out your therapist had no patient before you and therefore is fresh and awake and maybe even has had time to reread her notes about you and look out the window to see what kind of car you drive. We are afforded the illusion that the fertility clinic has nothing better to do today than carefully thaw our semen sample and insert it into my uterus. There are no other couples sizing us up, no one else's fertility is taking precedence over our own.

In the examining room I sign off that I have confirmed my name, date of birth, and Baldie's donor number. The nurse informs us that Baldie's sperm is especially good today—good motility, good counts, everybody swimming in the right direction. She writes "A+" on the slip of paper that contains Baldie's stats and gives it to me for good luck. Five minutes later I'm putting my pants back on.

This time Faith and I have a date. No more walking to the parking lot in silence and crying in the car around the block. This time we're going out for lunch and then for a long walk through Cambridge and Harvard Square. Not exactly a trip to Hawaii, but close enough.

Going to any public place after being inseminated is like having a dirty little secret, dirtier even than going out after sex, closer perhaps to just having had sex with a total stranger—which in some very unexciting scientific way I sort of have. Actually with two strangers, the sperm donor and the nurse. While Faith watched. We are procreating sluts sitting at a table as a bored-looking waitress hands us each a menu.

The terrible thing about playing your trump card is that it might not work. In some way Faith and I both have decided that by swallowing our ambivalence and ordering up two IUI's, by accepting the sacrifices of parenthood and taking on the challenges of the fertility clinic, by declaring ourselves ready, we have leapt the last hurdle and there is nothing left but for me to finally get pregnant. We are secretly convinced this month is it. So if I'm not pregnant, this will be the most devastating month of all. We toast a fragile little toast with our water glasses. Afterward, Faith points to my place mat, where a tiny rainbow is being reflected by the afternoon light.

The next morning, the fertility center is jam-packed with heterosexual couples, which is a total surprise because on the weekend the waiting room is usually chock-full of lesbians. The Fenway Community Health Center, which caters to most of the area's procreating lesbians, is closed for inseminations on the weekends, and so all sisters in the throes of ovulation are forced over to our fertility clinic. We were expecting something akin to a Melissa Etheridge concert. Instead it's the Dave Matthews holiday tour. Despite all of my "issues" with the lesbian nation, I have to admit I'm a bit disappointed. At the moment we open the waiting room door and everyone glances up from their issues of *Time* or *Newsweek* or *Parenting,* it's nice to see some familiar faces, rather than blank stares or utter incomprehension.

Faith and I decide to sit next to the most progressive-looking of all the heterosexuals, a young couple reading large hardcover books instead of magazines. She, with her long hippie brown hair, could easily teach women's studies. He, unshaven and in a Peruvian knit sweater, must have an ex-girlfriend or a sister who's a lesbian. The man and woman raise their eyes, glance at each other, and smile at us. *Look, lesbians!* I get the feeling our presence somehow turns their routine visit to the fertility clinic into a hip sociological adventure, similar to spending a week in a monastery or living for a month among chimpanzees.

Still, that's better than the confused stares from the other couples. One woman sitting clutching her husband's hand seems to be chanting a silent rosary: "There but for the grace of God go I."

I'm feeling bitchy this morning, not in the mood for another uterine intrusion, not in the mood to be "other." I want to lean into the terrified woman and say, "We may be your worst fear, lady, but we'll see who gets pregnant first!"

Faith refuses to remove her ski hat because she's cold and her hair is dirty, and I don't even care. Go ahead, wear a ski hat. Roll a joint. Pick your teeth with an amethyst crystal. So much for giving a shit about what the people at the fertility clinic think of us. So much for romance and special occasions.

We bury our heads in magazines, an ear out for the parade of nurses periodically poking their heads in to call out a client's name. "Marion?" "Susan?" When Nurse "I hit a brick wall" comes into the waiting room I feel my stomach muscles clench.

Faith's face goes white. "It's her."

We have linked all of the trauma of the last month to this nurse, who casually jabbed a catheter through my cervix and into my uterus and then claimed to have hit a brick wall rather than some unfortunate internal organ. We blame her for my not having gotten pregnant, for our fight in the car, for Eric the houseguest staying too long, for my mother's failed chemotherapy, and for my having gotten the flu.

Fortunately, "I hit a brick wall" looks down at the chart in her hand and calls, "Sarah?"

Within seconds an African-American woman bounds from her chair saying, "That's me."

Faith and I exchange glances and breathe one big simultaneous sigh of relief. Then, as the double doors close behind them, something horrifying happens. The women's studies professor next to us leans forward and says softly, though with adequate concern, "I'm Sarah too." The book in her lap falls closed. Clearly, she wants to jump from her chair and insist that the African-American woman might, in fact, be the wrong Sarah, while she, white Sarah, is the right one. But she can't. It's an awful dilemma for a politically correct women's studies professor sitting next to two lesbians at a fertility clinic. She looks to her husband, who shakes his head that all will be well—a premier Boston fertility clinic could not possibly make that kind of mistake—and goes back to his reading. But the women's studies professor no longer can concentrate on her book. She keeps straining her neck to try to see through the windows in the double doors, waiting for "I hit a brick wall" either to eject African-American Sarah or to come out and assure white Sarah that they are on top of it and the right Sarah will get the right sperm.

"Wow," Faith and I say in unison. Wowee.

Faith is convinced the Sarahs are in trouble, that each is going to be injected with sperm from the other's supply. She wants to tell the women's studies professor to do something, quick, before her husband passively impregnates another woman. My girlfriend loves a disaster. She loves snowstorms and earthquakes and hurricanes, anything that unites strangers and equalizes the common man or woman. I can tell she wants to lean over and offer advice to the women's studies professor and her husband, wants to chat it up with them like we are waiting together at Sears Automotive.

I remind Faith that women come here for reasons other

than to have an IUI. They come for blood tests and ultra-sounds. So maybe there's no chance of cross-pollination. Besides, I'm sure this couple, she being a women's studies professor and he a psychologist or an environmental engineer, can figure out for themselves the risk of sitting on their politically correct asses.

In her increasing agitation the women's studies professor lifts her eyes to us, woman-to-woman, her expression an unequivocal, "Jesus fucking Christ."

Within seconds another nurse throws open the double doors, "Sarah?"

Holy smokes.

The women's studies professor springs forth, "Which Sarah do you mean? I'm Sarah. Another Sarah went in when the other nurse said Sarah, but maybe that was supposed to be me. Which Sarah do you want?"

Just as we learn that the Sarahs indeed have been mixed up, switched, inverted, a cheerful nurse pops her head in and says, "Harlyn?"

Faith and I grab our things and gallop off, reluctant to miss the resolution of this drama, but thrilled to be free, if only for five minutes, from one of the many unpredictable hurdles on the journey to parenthood. Finally there is an obstacle we don't need to worry about. No one will ever confuse my name with that of another patient. We may be the only lesbians in the clinic today, but at least we're getting the right sperm!

The Bay in Winter

(SIBLING RIVALRY, TRANSFERENCE, AND AH, WELL, BLOODY HELL)

It's official. My younger sister is *trying* to get pregnant.

I dream I'm doing a little "work" on the living room wall in my childhood home in New Jersey. While my parents host a dinner party on the other side of the room, I begin by taking down pictures, the nails and hooks that they hang on. And then the paint begins to peel and the wall itself crumbles, until I'm brushing away dust and bits of Sheetrock to reveal cinder blocks and studs. I'm breathing in all of the dust and paint chips. My mother says from the couch on the other side of the room, "I really hope you know how to put this back together."

"Sure, I do."

I'm thinking I will have to go to Home Depot and buy Sheetrock. I wonder if it'll fit in my car. And aren't you supposed to tape seams or something? Shit. Then the worst thing of all occurs to me. This is my childhood house from the '60s, so of course the paint contains lead and in my dream I'm pregnant and have been breathing it all in, lead paint and paint dust and all sorts of other crap. I'm terrified. My unborn child will have fetal lead poisoning. I go into the bathroom and find my nostrils caked with lead paint dust.

Suddenly, I'm engaged in conversation with the music director of the arts program where I teach writing to children. The music director interrupts our conversation to tell me that she and one of the drama instructors have been talking and have decided they need to tell me something.

"Sure. Go ahead."

"You know, Harlie, since you're pregnant, you really should be careful about breathing in lead paint dust."

In therapy tomorrow, if I wanted to, I could discuss how I'm tearing down the walls of my childhood, dismantling all that did not work in my parent's house and rebuilding it for myself and my own family. It's dangerous work, and I'm not sure if I can do it without unintentionally endangering myself and my child. Instead, I more than likely will ask my therapist if she's happy to see me because her face will be so somber and serious that it'll seem as if she would rather be roasting in hell than sitting across from me at 7:30 in the morning. And when she asks why it matters whether or not she is happy to see me, I will want to spring from my chair and shake her with both my hands. Instead I will say, "It doesn't matter." So there. And then we will discuss whether or not I want to start therapy again after my hiatus, which will lead to a conversation about money. Maybe, maybe at the three-minute mark I might bring up the walls, and then, of course, it will be time to go. I will schedule another session because it will feel that we are right in the middle of something. That is how I keep myself in therapy.

It could be anything, my period due in a week (or not), the fact that our cat likes to walk on my chest, pushing down heavily with each paw as if compressing grapes into wine, but anyway, the thing is my breasts hurt. A little. They don't usually start to hurt this long before my period. Granted, it could be psychological, the power of the mind. This, of course, is what I know to expect. But I don't remember it happening the other four times.

And all of these strange psychic things have been happening (or all of these normal things that I interpret to be strange psychic things) like the rainbows and the night while lying in bed I told myself I was not pregnant and then closed my eyes to see a small yellow orb amid the blackness, floating there like an IMAX special adventure of what is going on inside my womb.

And Simone.

Every night before going to bed, Tory sings her a good-night song. It's the atheist's version of an evening prayer. They run through the names of everyone they know and love and wish them good night. Good night, Gran and Papa. Good night, Margaret, Beth, and baby Phoebe. Good night, Harlie, Faith, and George.

But "Good night, Harlie?!" Simone shouted the other night. "Good night, Harlie! Harlie's going to have a baby!"

Crazy. If I'm not pregnant this time, I'm fucked. Or I should be.

I wake up two mornings in a row with an upset stomach. Is this it? Is this pregnancy?

My period is due in four days. My breasts no longer hurt, and my stomach is no longer upset.

Thanks to daily meditation, needle-hair acupuncture is a much more relaxing event. Now when Martha leaves me lying there with needles poking out of my "conception meridian," I follow my breath in and out and don't obsess over the financial status of celebrities. In and out, in and out. I'm doing well until Martha steps in to check on me and immediately I wonder if there's such a thing as a "financial meridian." It's like my mind has to quickly squeeze in a thought while it can, before I slam the door on it again. In and out. In and out. I picture my mind to be a puppy or a toddler or Faith. Mommy cannot pay attention to you now. You need to play by yourself. And it makes me so sad. Poor mind. Okay, just one little thought, let's hear it. What if I already am pregnant and the needles overstimulate my meridian? Could I miscarry? I wonder if Martha has ever slept with another woman. Haven't all herbal practitioners explored their bisexuality? Is she attracted to me? Am I attracted to her? I think I'm attracted to anyone who touches me, with the exception of my primary care palomino. And I most certainly am not attracted to any of the technicians or nurses at the fertility clinic. I definitely have been attracted to my therapist and to the Buddhist nun at the meditation center. Interestingly enough, I've never been attracted to any of my parents' friends. That probably has to do with the incest taboo. In, out. In, out.

It begins with pain, a dull ache and then a kind of deep pressure, like the earth's magnetic forces are drawing all of my internal organs slowly downward into her core. The pain wakes me from a sound sleep. Day twenty-five and here it is? My period? But there's no blood. And in the morning still no blood. The cramps go away. That afternoon my breasts hurt and I am so tired I do the hyper neurotic's most unthinkable act, I lie down and take a nap.

I decide that my uterus is opening up, letting go of fear and ambivalence to accept new life, to allow an embryo to implant. It is the battle of old versus new. It's the beginning. I rest. Eat. Try to make myself a welcoming host.

The next day, Faith and I drive to the beach in Provincetown. The bay in winter is still as glass. We hold hands on the shore at sunset and make a wish for our unborn family. We introduce the budding life inside me to the bay and vice versa. We think of names.

That night the cramps return worse than ever, waking me again and causing me to fear I am having a tubal pregnancy. I wake Faith and ask her whether we should call a doctor, maybe rush to an emergency room. I check. No blood. Something is wrong. Something is terribly, terribly wrong. Faith pats my back and tells me not to worry. Is she right or does she just want to go back to sleep? The cramps persist. I try to determine whether they're localized to one side, whether they're excruciating. I'm sweating. My T-shirt clings to my damp back. I try lying on my back, my side, my stomach, but each new position intensifies the throbbing. It is only when I'm out of bed, walking barefoot on the cold tile floor of the bathroom, that the cramps go away. I suppose that means it's not a tubal pregnancy. In my sleepy mind I tell myself, *It's not a tubal ligation. I'm not having a tubal ligation.*

Back to bed and the sensation slowly inches back until

finally it swells to an awful crescendo of heat and pain and pressure. I'm afraid I will die, die in this bed at age thirty-nine because I'm too timid to call an emergency room, because my girlfriend hates having her sleep interrupted. What a waste. I'm so young. In a world aside from that of trying to get pregnant I am still so young. And then the anesthesia. If this is a miscarriage or a tubal pregnancy I'll have to have general anesthesia and a D&C and maybe I'll lose a tube or an ovary or maybe my entire uterus. I can feel it now, like something is about to burst or explode. Appendicitis of the reproductive system. I squirm. I sweat. I picture myself being called by nurses out from the deep haze of general anesthesia, "Harlyn? Harlyn?" Someone patting my leg. The queasiness, the cracker, the ginger ale. I heard recently on National Public Radio that there's a shortage of anesthesiologists. Maybe after I learn I no longer can be a mother, I will go back to medical school to become an anesthesiologist. It will give me something to do. It will distract me from the hysterectomy that will leave me old at thirty-nine because I lay in bed too long in pain.

I take another walk on the cold tiles, sit down on the toilet, and check one more time. Ah. Blood.

It's because we were so certain this time, wanted it so bad, that a tubal pregnancy, an emergency hysterectomy, even death, seemed more likely than the fact that I simply might not be pregnant, that, after all, I was just getting my period.

Resurrection

(PHEROMONES, NEANDERTHALS,
AND A WHOLE LOT OF SELF-HELP)

In the morning Faith hugs me and says she feels so sad and guilty.

"Guilty?"

"It's my fault."

She thinks that the arrival of her period a couple of days ago caused my hormones to roll off track, that her pheromones seduced my hormones away from motherhood and implantation, thereby forcing a little fertilized embryo out of my uterus and down the drain.

I laugh. It's so omnipotent, so pro-life a theory. But could it be? While during most of our seven and a half years together our cycles never have coincided, in the last two or three months we have started to get our periods at the same time. Could there be some validity to the idea that Faith's menstruating hormones shifted my own away from pregnancy? But why would my hormones just sit back and take it and not put up a fight? Why would hers suddenly kick in just to fuck me—or unfuck me, as the case may be? Could it be a biological manifestation of her ambivalence? Could we actually be engaged in a form of biological warfare? And then why would my hormones be the followers and Faith's the leaders?

"That's impossible," I tell her.

"You think so?"

Surely women have lived together for centuries with one sister or daughter or mother getting pregnant while another does not. Think of shtetls and caves and college dormitories.

"Definitely," I say. "Definitely not possible."

Meanwhile, I am crushed. Barren. Half a woman. I think maybe I can't get pregnant because deep down I'm not a good person. I have a withholding and hostile nature. I don't hold doors open for people who are more than five steps away. For instance, I don't pause and wait to hold open the door to our building at work, to ATM machines. If holding open the door means simply slowing my pace then I will do it, but I will not *stop* and *wait* for someone. And sometimes if I see someone I know coming toward me on the sidewalk or in a store, I pretend not to see them so that I won't have to smile and say hello because sometimes I just fucking hate smiling and saying hello. If I am just stepping out for a cup of coffee or to put a quarter in a meter it does not necessarily mean I'm in search of a good time—a smile and a conversation—so I'll pretend not to see him or her, whomever might require me to climb the cavernous walls of my psyche up and out of myself. So I'm not inherently nice. And I'm moody, prone to sullen mornings or angry afternoons. At those times even a sneeze or a cough in my direction can set me off. So I'm a freak as well. And I can't really picture myself pregnant, cannot imagine my stomach protruding so largely from my body that I have to look in a mirror to see my own pubic hair. I'm used to being able to see my pubic hair and my feet whenever I want to. Whenever the spirit moves me I might look down and take a peek. So I can hardly imagine not being able to do so, and that makes me a self-centered pervert incapable of sharing my body with a fetus, incapable of pregnancy and motherhood. And I'm thirty-nine-years-old and never even thought about whether I wanted to be a mother until relatively recently, so what do I expect? Some women have been working on this for years. Who am I to wake up one day in the twilight of my reproductive years, another woman by my side, and decide, hmm, I think I'll become a mother now? I am different. I have always felt different, and maybe this is it, this is why, because I am no mother, no mother am I.

I am back on litter box duty, and it seems the kitty has been saving up all of his poop just for me. Faith catches me staring inside the box at a pile so big the kitty should take a picture of it and submit it somewhere for a prize. Faith generously offers to continue being the sole scooper. But her charity makes me even sadder.

"No," I say. "I like it."

After shit patrol I'm on my way to work.

It is an awful, disgusting day. Overnight our snowy sidewalk has frozen solid to become what we tremulously refer to as the path of death. I have to walk without lifting my feet in order to get from the front door to my car without falling. As if I wasn't feeling badly enough about myself and the fitness of my anatomy, shuffling along in a bloated down coat and wool hat causes my already fragile sense of self to plummet even further into the bowels of hell. I am like a Neanderthal, angry and hunched over, dragging my knuckles on the ground and showing my teeth whenever anyone tries to pat me. I should be in a cage. I could sit in a corner with a bowl of food on my head, hurling hardened balls of my own shit at whomever provokes me. Instead I have to walk the path of death and go to work. Back when we were convinced I was pregnant, Faith meticulously sanded the sidewalk every day so that baby and I wouldn't tumble and fall. I slide one infertile foot in front of the other and think, I must remind her to save her energy. Let me fall.

The ride to work is an icy labyrinth of exhaust (no reason to worry about breathing that in anymore), traffic, and pedestrians, ninety-nine percent of whom are mothers with children. At noon my sister phones from Los Angeles to tell me about a Web site where if you punch in your birth date and the date you conceived your child you can find out whether you're going to have a girl or a boy.

"You would have had a girl," she says with a sigh.

Tortureyoursister.com.

We each want to name a child after our grandmother. Whoever has a girl first will win. If my grandmother knew of this race she would put her hand to her heart and say, "I'll kill myself." That was her response to any emotionally overwhelming and impossible situation, like when my sister and I lined up before her in little pink party dresses to ask, "Who do you like better?"

"I'll kill myself."

After my sister's heartwarming call, a writer friend phones to tell me she's written a short story about an American couple so desperate to have a child that while traveling in India they decide to accept an Indian couple's offer to sell them their newborn baby. In a back alley somewhere in Bombay the American husband pulls out a pile of rupees only to be robbed and then stabbed and killed by a gang of men. His wife is raped and murdered. Her dying words: "What if I'm pregnant?"

"Not at all hostile," I say to my friend, an Indian woman who just has found out that she's pregnant.

"It's not hostile!" She hates when I analyze things, when I refer to as "hostile" innocent remarks, creative story lines, or food that's too spicy for me to eat.

"Murder, rape, and infertility," I tell her. "It's the American nightmare jackpot."

"Americans are too sensitive. It's not like I mentioned the falling Dow."

I change the subject by telling her my sad story, how I'm menstruating and my doctor is a pig. My friend does the telephone equivalent of grabbing me by the shoulders and shaking me until I snap out of the awful funk.

"You must never ever go back to Dr. $," she implores. "You must find a new doctor and have an ultrasound and maybe a blood test. You must be able to talk with someone with empathy about what steps you should take next. You must do all of it in twelve days in time to inseminate again."

"Get mad," she says, and "Sorry for killing off the Americans."

"Oh, they probably deserved it."

I close my office door and call five doctors, including the kitty's: my gynecologist, my internist, Dr. $'s office, and a gynecologist a friend recommended long ago, a doctor with a reputation for being competent and kind and performing IUI's. And then I say a little prayer for myself in which I promise to remain good to myself, to continue to do all of the good things I've been doing to prepare myself for pregnancy: meditation, yoga, acupuncture. I will do them regardless. Loving yourself, your body, unconditionally whether or not you get pregnant is good practice for loving a child, whether or not he or she has broken a vase that day or dented the car. I must continue to love and respect my body whatever the outcome.

By the end of the day a receptionist has taken pity on me and miraculously arranged an appointment with the new kind doctor for the day after tomorrow.

I fantasize that this new doctor will be a sensitive ally, willing to walk the steps with me before injectable hormone treatments. That she will attempt to remember my medical history, that she will not doubt whether Faith and I are capable of planning our own finances. If she isn't, I'm armed with the name of another ob-gyn.

Mothers

(The Vagina Garden and a New Game Plan)

There are as many old women here in this new doctor's waiting room as there are young women and somehow that's so reassuring, like the new doctor has kept all of these vaginas alive for all of these years, cultivated and tended them like a garden. She is not all youth and fertility, all hormones and insensitivity and fertility statistics. She is the keeper of vaginas fertile and infertile, young and old, gay and straight. A mother escorts her teenage daughter to reception. An old man waits with his wife. I wish Faith were here, but she had to work, and the appointment was such a last-minute miracle I couldn't turn it down. I know she'd like it here with all of this humanity. She could wear her hat and chat it up with the older women.

The new doctor is straight and cute. When my sister, Carrie, lived in Boston and worked as a preschool teacher, she had my new doctor's son in her class.

He said she's got "jiggly wiggly boobs," Carrie told me

the morning of my appointment. "But I hear she's a great obstetrician."

The cute new doctor hears my story. I try to stop imagining her jiggly wiggly boobs as I tell her my story, how Dr. $ is ready to inject me with hormones without doing any tests to make sure all systems are go, without taking any one of a number of other baby steps. I tell her how a year ago Dr. $ insisted I have surgery to have a uterine polyp removed then forgot about it and dismissed the idea of perhaps checking to see if the polyp had returned. I tell her how I'm nervous about taking hormones as my mother has ovarian cancer and there is some evidence, though perhaps unsubstantiated, that hormones to increase ovulation can increase a woman's risk of ovarian cancer. The new doctor shakes her head unequivocally and asks about my LH and estradiol levels.

"Excuse me?"

Apparently there's a very simple blood test I should have had before I even began trying to get pregnant. If these hormone levels, LH and estradiol, are too low then I won't be able to get pregnant, with or without injectable hormone treatment.

"What day of your cycle are you on?"

"Four."

"I'll get a blood sample today."

This is what I meant. This is what concerned me so, that Dr. $ would shoot me up with hormones for no reason at all, without first checking that everything else was okay, without first confirming that they, indeed, were warranted. Never mind the thousands of dollars we could have wasted on sperm and inseminations and nitrogen bomb tanks if for some reason my hormone status is Shitsville.

The new doctor also suggests I have a hysterosalphingogram, or HSG, as soon as possible. She explains that an

HSG is like the barium enema of reproductive technology. Dye is inserted into your uterus and then its journey through your reproductive system, specifically your fallopian tubes, is tracked by an X-ray. It enables a competent and proactive doctor to look at your uterus and fallopian tubes and make sure there are no polyps or other such obstacles, that your tubes are clear, and that overall you are in proper physiological shape to become pregnant.

The new doctor reads the expression on my face: a medley of disbelief and rage.

"I'm just doing what you want," she tells me. "I'm just listening to you."

I want to know why, why didn't Dr. $ do these procedures? Even following the logic of big business and profit, it seems one would want to do all they could to see if a patient can even get pregnant prior to administering drugs and adding her long list of failed pregnancies to their precious statistics.

Unfortunately, the new doctor no longer performs inseminations. I still will need to go to a fertility clinic to have that procedure done. At this point the thought of going back to Dr. $ and her office is repugnant. I hate her. I don't trust her. If she weren't a lesbian herself I would think she had been discriminating against us, had been trying to get rid of Faith and me and our hippie lezzie fantasy of having a baby. But she is gay, and her bull mastiff of a medical resident was butcher than the men who work on our cars. So I am baffled, totally baffled.

"You should know that not all fertility clinics will work with single women," the new doctor tells me.

"I'm not single."

Apparently, women seeking to get pregnant without a

husband or boyfriend are considered "single" by the medical establishment. Because you can claim not to accept single women clients, but you cannot say you will not accept lesbians.

It's like finding out there's no Santa Claus, like learning at age thirty that you were adopted or your parents have other children. I may not be able to be inseminated because I'm not *married*? It's crazy and naive and blind of me, but I'm totally and utterly shocked. A fertility clinic would turn down my money because I'm gay? Isn't that illegal? Isn't there something in the Hippocratic oath that forbids denying health care to gays and lesbians? Isn't that a form of genetic engineering? I keep running into this again and again, but because being gay is so much just part and parcel of the whole picture, not number one on the list of who I am, sometimes I honestly truly forget about it. And sometimes I forget that anyone else would even notice or care. What does some anonymous medical center care about whether I am gay or straight? Suddenly I realize the vast and crucial importance of places like the Fenway Community Health Center, a medical clinic that caters to gay clients, of community centers and softball teams and potlucks.

The new doctor informs me that our repugnant fertility clinic is one of the few in town that has no problem treating "single women," that that is where she would refer a client trying to get pregnant without a male partner. There is another clinic, however, that she thinks is great. "Call them and see if they take 'single women.'"

I'm not single.

"If they can't do it sooner, then I'll do the HSG this Monday."

It's Thursday afternoon. Of course no one else will be able to see me to do a consult and then perform an HSG before Monday. Perhaps it is this new doctor's way of telling me she will be there for me, that she will listen, and that Dr. $ is indeed fucked-up. I am so eternally grateful, and probably because I am gay, that makes me think again about her jiggly wiggly boobs.

It's exhausting. Overload. Medical madness. There are too many doctors in our life. Between my mother's illness and my trying to get pregnant, in the last year we have had cause to visit all of the major hospitals in the Boston area, Beth Israel/Deaconess, Brigham and Women's, Dana-Farber, the bastard fertility clinic. We were never like this before. We were not a medical family. We had our yearly check-ups and then went our healthful ways. To think we had believed that my getting pregnant would be a welcome distraction from all things medical, from waiting rooms and specialists and blood tests, from X-rays and I.V.'s. If nothing else, I suppose all of this has reduced going to the dentist to the most minor of nuisances. There's nothing like a major medical adventure to put teeth cleaning and gingivitis in perspective.

I leave this message on the receptionist's voice-mail at the new fertility clinic: "Hi, I'm calling to see if you accept *single* women patients. I'm not really single, but I understand that's the term you use to refer to lesbians. I have a partner, but he is a she. Anyway, we've been disappointed with our present fertility clinic and would like a second opinion, but only if you are willing to work with us. I heard not all fertility clinics are willing to work with same-sex couples. That was a surprise. I don't know why not. Anyway, my number is…"

Our friends Margaret and Beth want us to get together with them and their five-month-old daughter, Phoebe. Phoebe, the biological daughter of Margaret and donor number 4578, has blond hair and blue eyes. Sometimes she looks like Margaret and sometimes you can tell she's looking exactly like somebody else, only we have no idea who. I think less of her donor father at these times than I do of his mother. Imagine knowing you had a grandchild somewhere with golden hair like your son and the same furrow to her brow as the one you wiped clean when he was just a baby. So many of the donors are young men without children of their own and therefore have no way of knowing what it's like to see themselves in a baby or a toddler, to see a piece of their brother or sister or the grandfather that they held dear reflected in new life. I think that if they could imagine this, if they had had this experience, many of them probably would not choose to donate.

But a mother knows. And it's the mothers of the donors that cause me the most sadness and perhaps the most concern. I bet very few if any donors tell their parents they're selling their semen for money, that they might sire up to ten offspring with up to ten different women, none of whom they may ever meet. Always it leads me to imagine this disastrous scenario: A young man dies tragically young. His parents are heartsick to lose their son, especially before he had a chance to know the joys of fatherhood himself, before leaving an heir in his place. But then somehow, through a loose-lipped friend or a file left on his nightstand, the young man's parents find out that he had donated sperm and that, in fact, he does have children! Only the children, their grandchildren, are scattered across the country and beyond their reach. What is a desperate devastated mother (or father or both) left to do? Find those kids! Hire a lawyer and fight the current donor laws! Make it the new guiding light in their lives. And if they do manage to find their biological grandchildren at home with two lesbian moms, what then??

Meanwhile, we have dinner with Margaret and Beth and baby Phoebe. Margaret seems tired but ecstatic; Beth mostly seems fatigued. They tell stories of the downfalls of what at first seems to be two-mother parenting but later reveals itself to be more related to the fact of two people raising a child who is only biologically related to one of them. While Margaret's family came immediately from the West Coast to visit their new grandchild, Beth's mother and sisters have yet to visit. Beth thinks it isn't clear to them that Phoebe is their relation even though Beth is one of Phoebe's legal parents, even though she's up all night with Phoebe and takes care of her every day, even though Phoebe will call her "Mom." As with any form of misunderstanding or lack of regard that befalls a gay couple, it is easy to lay blame on homophobia, on the fact that Beth and Margaret are two women living together. If Beth and her husband had just adopted a baby, would Beth's mother and sisters feel differently? Would they consider the child to be more Beth's and therefore more a grandchild because Beth was the only mother, or because the relationship between two parents to an adopted child is more or less equal, at least from a biological perspective, or because Beth was raising a child with a man?

It would remain impossible to know except that Beth's mother eventually came right out and said, "I want *you* to have a baby."

"But I *do* have a baby," Beth says, cradling Phoebe in her arms.

Thankfully neither of them brings up the idea of swapping donor numbers.

The new fertility clinic calls back. Of course they would be willing to work with us.

"I'm also really not interested in aggressive treatment at this point. I mean, I've only had four IUI's and already our other doctor wants to inject me with hormones without even checking to see if there's some other problem."

"That's fine."

"I think there are probably other steps we could take before that."

"That's right."

"All right, then."

"All right."

The HSG

(LAVENDER WASHES AND ISN'T IT ROMANTIC TAKE FOUR)

It's Monday morning the day of the HSG, the day lab results come back, the day we find out whether I have a fertility problem. Faith has workshops scheduled all day, so my friend Tory, Simone's mother, will be escorting me to the hospital. With all of our involuntary hospital visits, it is odd to be going voluntarily. My mother offered to go, but I couldn't bear another trip to the hospital with my mother. It's too sad to be sitting in hospital waiting rooms with my mom, too reminiscent of past traumas, of traumas yet to come. That, and how could I sit nervously awaiting a simple injection of dye into my uterus when my mother is gearing up to have chemotherapy poured into her liver?

"Let's go out for dinner instead," I suggest. Let's spend time together doing anything but sitting anxiously in a hospital, even though her impulse is sweet and good, a way of transcending her own illness by reaching out to take care of her daughter.

I make myself a cup of tea and consider the fact that if I had no desire to become pregnant I could be at work right now. I remind myself that work is not the greatest place in the world to be, and being there indefinitely without any plans for enriching my future (i.e., becoming a mother) is an empty, uninspiring alternative. Still, I'm scared.

In honor of today's photo session with my uterus and fallopian tubes I dreamed last night that I was underwater, swimming through a tight tunnel, holding my breath as long as I could as I pushed my way along, desperate to get to open air. There were unexpected obstacles in the way, including a dead body (!) and passages too narrow to swim through without scraping my face. After finally breaking surface in a vast and sprawling ocean, I suddenly was riding shotgun with my father in a rental car, trying to find a place to return the car that didn't involve going to an airport.

It's a good thing doctors don't mention things like four-inch novocaine needles that will be inserted into your cervix and extra-large freezing-cold speculums that will wrench open your narrow lesbianic vagina, when suggesting you undergo a routine medical procedure such as an HSG. It's a good thing you see the four-inch novocaine needle for the first time when you're lying half-naked on your back, legs up in stirrups, and therefore not in a position to bolt the fuck out the door. It's a good thing that the cervix doesn't have much feeling and that time passes, so that all four-inch needles inserted into your cervix eventually are withdrawn. Otherwise, no woman in her right mind would arrive on time for such a procedure, joke with the receptionist, and then walk willingly down the hall to shed her clothes.

The procedure itself isn't nearly as awful as the thought of a four-inch needle going into your cervix. A four-inch needle going into your cervix is not as awful as the *thought* of a four-inch needle going into your cervix. It goes like this. There's your gynecologist standing between your legs manipulating a large metal rod that she or he has inserted through your anesthetized cervix and into your unanesthetized uterus. At the end of the rod is a balloon that your gynecologist will inflate whenever he or she is commanded to squirt toxic dye into you by the radiologist. It's not clear which causes the pain, the dye or the balloon. Either way, the result is the distressing sensory combination of menstrual cramps and the desire to shit your brains out on the table. The radiologist, aside from giving orders to your gynecologist, will instruct you to roll to your left side and then your right side and then down on your back again, the better for he or she to X-ray you and watch the dye as it— hopefully—follows an easy course from your uterus through your fallopian tubes. There's a nurse present for the sole purpose of patting your shoulder or your knee. And then there's the television screen where the whole party going on inside of you is broadcast live like an NBC special report. "Harlyn Aizley's reproductive system is brought to you this afternoon by Monistat-7. To say the least, it works on yeast! Now back to our show."

The terminus will be pronounced by the radiologist's offhand remark, "It's in the gut," which means the dye has traveled its course and the show's over. The radiologist will have exited before you even realize there no longer is a metal pole hanging out of your vagina. Then your new gynecologist, the one who you like so much, will say, "You did great," and the nurse will hand you a washcloth and instruct you to go into the bathroom and wipe the blood and dye from between your legs.

That night, for some reason, you will dream of the Statue of Liberty, a stoic French woman with a torch.

The results are in. My hormone levels are fine, but my right fallopian tube may be blocked. Instant replay revealed that dye started to flow through my right tube and then stopped. The new doctor explains this could be due to an obstacle in its path or to the fact that the whole process of dye being squirted through a fallopian tube can cause it to spasm.

I have 148 questions. I want to know how we find out whether or not the tube really is blocked. And what exactly blocks a tube? What could possibly be in there? I want to know if I should inseminate only every other month, if I should have ultrasounds to predict which side I am ovulating on.

The nice doctor refers me and all of my questions to the new doctor.

All along, one of our upstairs lesbians, Margaret, has been waxing poetic about "the wash." "Have a wash," she says. "It's a nice way to open up your tubes."

I imagine the wash involves water scented with lavender and rose petals that is flushed through you via an entirely biodegradable tube, perhaps a hose made of sea vegetables and soy. Women with messy braids or long-flowing dread-locks hum as they gently insert the tube and prepare to flush out your womanhood, a process that has the advantage of causing a spiritual awakening and maybe a vision or two of your fertile female ancestors.

I run into Margaret the day after the HSG. She's holding

baby Phoebe in her arms, the two of them cooing like pigeons. "You know," she says. "My doctor thinks IUI's are most successful immediately following a wash."

"Thank you very much," I tell Margaret. "But I cannot tolerate a 'wash' right now. I've just had my entire reproductive system snaked and drained." I tell her about the needles and the toxic dye and the spasms.

"That's the wash!" Margaret says, smiling.

"That's what you've been calling a wash?"

"Sure," she says. Baby Phoebe gurgles in confirmation.

That's why Margaret got pregnant and I haven't, because she refers to an HSG as "a wash" rather than as a trip through reproductive hell, because she sees her uterus as half full and I see mine as half empty.

Still, despite the blood and cramps, the potential log jam in my right tube, and the desire to lock my vagina closed for the next six months, I take her advice and schedule an IUI for later in the week. That gives me two to three more days of vaginal peace and the chance to drink a beer.

It is our last—we hope—trip to the terrible fertility clinic. We go in ready for bear but find it is a happy, friendly Saturday. The heterosexual couples in the waiting room are smiling and talkative. In the exam room the nurse has all the time in the world to spend with us and answer our questions. After she completes the deed she pats my knee with her gloved hand and says, "Maybe this one is it."

Fifteen days later I'm bleeding like a stuck pig.

Truth Is Always Stranger Than Fiction

(HAMSTERS AND A BOATLOAD OF JUSTICE)

It's just that I have spent the last four and a half years watching my mother battle ovarian cancer. It's just that I work in medical research and know that even unsubstantiated theories are theories, that ideas come from *somewhere*. Not everything exists as an unsubstantiated scientific finding. Some things don't worry us at all. For example, nobody is doing research on the potential link between saltines and ovarian cancer, between classical music and ovarian cancer, between Tylenol and ovarian cancer. So, as we gear up to help my mother survive yet another debilitating round of chemo, I find it harder than ever to consider taking fertility hormones that have even the slightest shadow of association with you-know-what. If there's no other way to get pregnant, I will do it. (Wouldn't it be awful to decide not to have a baby because I don't want to take hormones that might cause cancer and then wind up getting cancer anyway?) I will take them if I have to. But before I do, there's one thing I need to know. I want to know whether our sperm donor has gotten anybody else pregnant. Maybe Faith was right. Maybe it's not me.

I call the woman at the sperm bank—our old friend from the days of the nitrogen bomb tank and the soldiers and New Jersey and "Jews sell out fast"—and ask her my big question.

"I was just wondering," I say, because it's months later, and since we didn't buy all of Baldie's remaining Jewish vials, someone else must have. "Have any other women gotten pregnant from donor number 232?"

The woman pauses before responding, "Funny you should ask."

Funny you should ask?

Apparently just a few moments ago, this very same morning, another woman called to ask the very same question about the very same donor. And then there was the woman back in October who sold her vials because she couldn't get pregnant and instead had chosen to adopt. And those are just the women we know about.

It feels as if the floor in my kitchen is dipping and swaying, like the walls have come alive. Everything seems to be moving without me. I grab the back of a chair to steady myself, to feel something solid in my potentially very fertile hands.

"So," I manage to say, "it seems there are three of us who have not gotten pregnant with the sperm of donor number 232."

"At least," says the woman at the sperm bank. "There are at least three of you. If you ask me, statistically, somebody should have gotten pregnant by now."

Holy fucking shit.

Whether or not the sperm bank would have called of
their own accord to tell us this information is an unan-
swerable question that's best not to ask. However, we are
asked that question seemingly every hour of every day by
concerned friends and family. Indeed, we ask it of each
other in the still of the night when we are trying to fall
asleep, in the kitchen while we are making dinner, amid the
bare trees when we are taking an evening walk.

Would they ever have told us?

When it rains it pours, and there's just way too much
going on right now: my mother on the verge of this brand-
new chemoembolization, a potentially "bad" sperm donor,
and Faith's car, which died this morning, for good. To top
it all off I've taken a new job teaching expository writing
because, apparently, my agent can no longer sell my writing. We're having an awful week, and since there's very little I can do about any of it, I decide I want to sue the sperm
bank. I want to arrive at their office in San Francisco like
Clint Eastwood in *Unforgiven* and take back the fucking
night, or at the very least, all our money.

Faith talks me out of it. We need our energy, she says.
Right now we need peace and harmony and sanity. We can
ask for our money back—$3,000—but we should focus our
energy on finding a new donor. We need to devote ourselves
to getting me pregnant, getting my mother through this procedure, finding another car. We kiss and hug and commend
each other for being so strong and resilient.

As soon as Faith leaves for work I call a lawyer. I have
to. I am a wronged Jew, the child of divorce. If I don't, I
might explode.

The sperm bank is taking a shady stance. While admitting

that Baldie should have gotten *somebody* pregnant by now, and while suggesting to us that we definitely should switch to a different donor, they still hesitate to admit there's something wrong (i.e., to refund our money). His counts were good, after all, the sperm strong and abundant, each of the million or so little guys swimming in the right direction. Never mind the fact that nobody was getting pregnant, that good sperm counts don't necessarily mean a thing, that thousands of women across the globe are undergoing extensive—and potentially dangerous—fertility treatments when, in fact, the problem is that the semen at their disposal is deeply and insidiously flawed.

"A hamster penetration test has not been performed," the woman explains. "But that test rarely is performed now anyway."

At first I don't really hear her, don't even register the fact that she has said "hamster," as in Sniffy, our class pet at Play House Nursery School, West Orange, N.J., circa 1964. All that sinks in is that there is another test, one that goes beyond the basic question of motility and counts and live and dead sperm swimming in the right direction. There is—or was—a test that asks another question, a male-fertility question, and it no longer is performed because it's too expensive or because it involves informing men that they are genetically impotent and it's just more tasteful to go on assuming that infertility is a woman's issue.

"It's an old test," she continues. "It goes beyond the standard measures for male infertility and tests whether the sperm is capable of penetrating an egg membrane."

Sounds good to me. Sounds appropriate. If I'm willing to have a three-foot novocaine needle inserted into my cervix to determine whether I'm fertile, I don't see why a vial of semen—far removed, I might add, from its source—should not undergo a painless analysis underneath a microscope by a...hamster?

"What does this have to do with hamsters?"

"Rather than harvest your eggs, the test is performed on a hamster egg. Hamster eggs are very similar to human eggs."

Speak for yourself.

"So would your lab perform this test?"

She doesn't think the director of the sperm bank will consent to the (expensive) test. However, if we have the test done here in Boston and it comes out positive, suggesting Baldie couldn't even impregnate a hamster, they will repeat it in San Francisco. At stake: our 3,000 bucks.

"Fine," I say. "We'll have the test done here in Boston." I have no idea who will perform this test or where that person will find an ovulating hamster, but I'm certain I won't stop searching until I find out. We have five more vials of Baldie's sperm in storage. I'll do the test myself if I have to, on a cat or a guinea pig or a goldfish from the pet store.

A day later the woman calls us back to tell us the director of the sperm bank has agreed to offer us a credit in the amount of the number of remaining vials we have of donor number 232. We can apply this credit to any other donor at the sperm bank.

I can't say that I'm comfortable with the idea of using another donor from this sperm bank. But starting from scratch, with consent forms and donor catalogs and hundreds, perhaps thousands of dollars, is an equally disquieting thought.

"What if we would rather have a refund?"

"Then you need to write a letter to the director explaining everything that has happened."

Let's see, for starters we have my using up six months of my dwindling fertile lifetime, the $3,000 we invested in Baldie, the six IUI's, the consultations with three different doctors, and the seven-foot novocaine needle. Not bad. Never ask a pissed-off writer to concoct such a letter.

"Just tell me who I should address it to."

Look out sperm bank, here I come.

Boot Camp

(New Cars, New Sperm, and a Chemoembolization)

The space station Mir is scheduled to crash into the Pacific Ocean after fifteen years in space. What a week, I tell you. Look out below!

Faith and I sit at the dining room table and make a list of all the things we need to get done in the next week. We need to see my mother through the chemo, get Faith a car, and find a new sperm donor. Faith takes the car project, I take the sperm donor and the letter. We will split getting my mother well three ways with my sister, who is due to arrive from Los Angeles in two days. We also must get to work, feed ourselves, and remember to bathe.

The hour-and-a-half chemoembolization takes three and a half hours because my mother's artery has a curve or a bend or an unexpected detour due to construction. Thankfully, nurses periodically emerge from radiology to update my sister and I on the progress. They know enough to smile as they make their way down the hall. They maintain fake, deliberate smiles the entire length of the hall, until they're close enough so that their words are audible. "She's doing fine." Then their facial muscles relax into bland indifference and they continue down the hall to the cafeteria or to the bathroom or to the outside lobby for a smoke.

My sister and I pass the time gossiping and eating Balance Bars. When finally our mother is wheeled out of radiology on a gurney, we are emotionally exhausted and she is in a deep drug-induced fog. The procedure, much like an angiogram, involves threading a tube up through an artery in her groin all the way into the left side of her liver and then injecting chemotherapy through the tube and into her liver. It's gone well. But "What a route we had to take!" the doctors and nurses keep saying. "What a detour." As if my mother, at some point in her life, had chosen to have her artery curved and tangled much like one might choose to have breast implants or a perm. They all keep shaking their heads and looking at our unconscious mother: "That's quite an artery!"

The next day at dawn, our mother is wheeled back to Radiology to have a CAT scan. The scan reveals that the doctors and nurses took the right detour. The chemo has filled the left side of her liver and penetrated the tumor. In three more weeks we will know if, in response, the cancer cells have waved a white flag and declared defeat. In the meantime, my mother will be too exhausted to take care of herself. Loads of liver cells are dead and apparently that can really wear a person down, not to mention the effects of the chemo. My sister and Faith and I arrive at the hospital after the CAT scan, in time to hear all of this news. We are instructed to cook for our mother and clean for her, to make sure she drinks two liters of fluid a day and that her temperature does not rise above 101. Then we gather my mother's belongings, load her into the car, and take her home.

Several friends with children have described returning home from the maternity ward with their newborn, opening the door to their home, looking at their partner, and thinking, "Now what the hell do we do?" It's much like that with our mother. She folds herself into the corner of her sectional sofa and closes her eyes. The three of us, not one of whom is a trained caregiver, exchange worried glances.

Carrie has the first shift: week one. We figure we'll play it by ear after that. The doctor has told us that our mother really will only need twenty-four-hour care for the first week. In three weeks she should be up and about. After Carrie returns to Los Angeles, my mother's younger brother will arrive for a four-day shift. That takes us to the weekend, when, free from work, I grab the baton and take my mother through Sunday, when, voilà!, ten days will have passed and she will be on her toes.

By 9 P.M. on the evening of my mother's first day home she's running a fever of 103. My sister and I bundle her into the car and spend the next five hours in an emergency room watching numbly as she receives two liters of I.V. fluids and much attention from nervous residents who seem to think that her heart rate of 180 beats per minute is a terrible thing. Fortunately, my sister and I don't realize how terrible a thing a heart rate of 180 is until the next day when a cardiologist explains why our mother will remain in the hospital under careful surveillance for at least two more days. Then we freak. We can't stop asking each other the horrible and unnecessary question, "What if we hadn't taken her to the emergency room? What if we hadn't taken her to the emergency room?" It's a useless, pointless, torturous question, but we play it over and over again for no reason other than to make ourselves sick. It reminds me of the time Simone kept pressing the repeat button on the stereo playing "You Are My Sunshine" over and over again to make herself cry.

"It's such a sad song, Mommy," she explained to Tory, who had come in to see why her three-and-a-half-year-old was sitting in front of the stereo sobbing.

I'm not sure if my sister and I want to cry like that, or somehow want to keep feeling the weight of what has happened, but we need to stop asking ourselves this question. We need to stop pressing the repeat button over and over and over again.

It's incredible how totally and utterly *over* are the days of looking for a Jewish donor. It's not just that there is not a decent Jew to be found in any of the sperm banks we are willing to use because we remain hell-bent on providing our children with a yes donor whom they can meet one day should they so desire and there are only two sperm banks in the nation that offer such an option (both of which seem to be running specials on Jews with mental illness)—it's not just that. Seeing how far our last Jew got us, I find myself wanting the seed of someone entirely different from him, from myself, from us. I imagine Baldie to have been so genetically similar to me as to be almost invisible, like part of the problem was that my eggs didn't even notice his passive little sperm were there. Like spoiled, lazy familiar brats they entered my womb, sat down, and waited for my eggs to make the first move. So, no way. I want foreign sperm,

sperm that shouts "I'm here!" and looks so utterly different from my Ashkenazi eggs that they perk up and take notice. I want action. And I want anyone I can find with a clean medical history.

Faith agrees. We communicate all of this via cell phones. Faith has a cell phone with her at the car dealership. My sister has one at the hospital, and I have one with me at the sperm bank library at the Fenway Community Health Center, in which are stored donor profiles from every sperm bank in California. All day long we trade information regarding my mother's heart rate, front-wheel-drive four-door sedans, and the medical histories of anonymous men.

The first problem is that our guilty sperm bank has offered us five free vials of new sperm, but not one of their other identity-release donors is in any way appealing. The tide has turned and suddenly it's slim pickins at the sperm orchard. The only men available seem to be right out of one of my research studies on the genetic components of mental illness: paternal uncles who've been hearing voices for twenty years, grandmothers who have jumped off cliffs. At least they are honest. Maybe it's the donors who deny any such history that we need to worry about. I pore over every profile the sperm bank has to offer, stretching our limits, erasing a standard here, a preference there. Does it really matter that not one of a donor's relatives has ever gone to college? Boston has a great medical community, so do we really need to be concerned that most of the males in another donor's family suffer from mild hemophilia? Still, I cannot squeeze one of them into the realm of possibility.

It seems there's no alternative but to switch sperm banks. That means lawyers and letters and all sorts of effort to obtain some other form of compensation aside from five free vials of psycho-sperm. Just one more item for the list: heal mom, find donor, buy car, threaten sperm bank.

But on the way from one file drawer to another, something catches my eye. It's a manila folder with Baldie's donor number on it. It's his medical profile, the one I dreamed the sperm bank sent us for free. I haven't seen it for months. I told myself I'd order it the moment I became pregnant. Then we would store it in some special baby file for our child to see in years to come. In my memory it says Baldie is kind and caring and loves to cook, that he donated sperm to help unfortunate couples who could not otherwise have children, that he is sweet and smart and talented.

What it really says is the reason he has decided to donate sperm is because it's a way for him to create offspring given that his wife can't get pregnant!

Motherfucker.

At the time it must have seemed so innocent an explanation; an educated man committed to his wife wants somehow to get his genes into the next generation. At least he had a committed relationship, at least he was literate, at least he was honest. Never had it occurred to us—or to the sperm bank—that *he* might be the reason his girlfriend could not conceive. His counts were good. It never crossed anyone's mind. Or did it?

It's slim pickins too at the only other sperm bank in the country to offer identity-release donors. There are about seven of them total at this bank, and that includes men of all races. There is one Jew who reports a family history of depression so pervasive that I feel my own serotonin levels dip just thinking about him. There's a man who suffers from what the sperm bank insists is a clinically insignificant penile irregularity, a man whose mother and father both were drug addicts, and a man who's made a living doing something with boxes and trucks and international borders that is just too mysterious for my taste. I find myself sneaking peeks at the profiles of "no" donors, men who will not allow their offspring to contact them. Would that really be so bad? Maybe laws will change by then or maybe the donor's mind will have changed. Maybe our children won't care.

I call Faith. "What about switching to a 'no' donor?" I explain that the country is filled with "no" donors. Maybe we're limiting ourselves to strange men and strange sperm banks by insisting we have a donor our child can someday meet.

Faith is sitting across the desk from a used-car salesman. I hear her say to him, "Give me one minute."

"We have to have a yes donor," she whispers into the phone. "It just doesn't seem right not to."

I remember. The yes donor was our compromise. It was the next best thing to Faith's first choice: a known donor. It is the middle ground, the place where we laid down our swords and shook hands. We have to remain on that territory. If we shift, we risk one of us forever resenting the other and a million years of couples counseling.

"Okay, but there's hardly anybody. How do you feel about social phobia?"

The car dealer interrupts with some vital information about alignment and warranties and body integrity. For a second I think he's referring to a sperm donor. I imagine sperm brokers, salesmen who sit down with you and bombard you with SAT scores, neuropsychological ratings, and hand size.

"Listen," the sperm salesman would say, "if you were my daughter I would insist you take donor number 9873. Personally," he'd lower his voice to a whisper, "I'd rather have a kid with social phobia than one who'd run out of the house not giving a damn about anything. Know what I mean?"

"Find one," Faith says.

Two days later, between visits to the cardiology unit and the sperm library, between conferences with doctors, interns, and nurses, I've found us a new sperm donor and Faith has found a new car. As luck would have it, both are Japanese.

I'd like to say that I was not at all swayed by the fact that our new donor is reported to be "extraordinarily good looking," that his looks did not cause me to overlook a little family history of alcoholism, high blood pressure, and Buddhism. I'd like to say that, but honestly I'm not sure. With Baldie there was always in the back of our mind the fear that on that day of days we would look through teary eyes across my swollen belly at a seven-pound six-ounce ugly bundle of joy. We would love our children one way or another, of course. Of course! And surely handsome genes don't guarantee you a thing, but they're a nice start. At least we would have seen the guy across a crowded room and murmured something positive. At least evolution would have been working in our favor. Besides, his medical history was the cleanest of any of the other identity-release donors. And that, I told myself, was why it didn't at all matter that he was half Dutch and half Japanese.

My mother's heart rate has dropped from 180 to 86, which in combination with the hope of a handsome new sperm donor is cause for major celebration. We are the luckiest family in the world! In addition, her fever is down to 101, and when I return from the sperm library she has just finished eating solid food!

My sister, on the other hand, looks wrecked. While I haven't slowed down long enough for my body to remember sitting in an emergency room until 3 A.M. as recently as two nights ago, my sister's body has caught up. She is pale and limp, mopey and unfriendly.

To cheer everybody up, I tell them—should all go well—we will have a new quarter-Japanese member of the family. They are thrilled. They too love the idea of new blood. In response to the events of the last week—the last few years—we finally can admit we are sick of ourselves. We are sick of being carriers of Tay-Sachs and cancer and anxiety. We want a break. We want the next generation to meditate and drink green tea in addition to eating borscht and matzoh ball soup. What's so great about maintaining the tribe? What matters most is love and health and family and getting pregnant.

We toast with water and I.V. fluids. Our luck has changed!

My mother is in the hospital for the next three days because her fever and her heart rate keep going up and down like a seesaw, like this is some new form of illness—neither sick nor well, just up and down and in-between. Our mother, who is usually so resilient that she spends the day after chemotherapy driving to and from Vermont, is down. She is exhausted and weak, angry and afraid, and that turns our world upside-down. There have been times during her fight with cancer that she has been healthier than any of us, and that, I now learn, has afforded us a great deal of denial. Even though the battle is almost five years old, she thus far has gone relatively unscathed and we have gone blissfully ignorant of the severity of her illness. But now, at night after visiting my mother, I dream of my grandmother after the stroke. It's all too familiar, the two of them just five years apart, skin and bones lying lifeless in a hospital bed.

And then on Sunday her fever is down, her heart rate has been regular for over five hours, she's drinking enough fluid so that the I.V. may be disconnected, so she's discharged home—again.

I decide it's good that I'm not pregnant, that this all has been way too stressful, that I should try to conceive during a month of calm—if there is such a thing. My sister insists everything is as it should be—my pregnantlessness, the course of my mother's recovery. My sister has become one of those "everything happens for a reason" people. She says this to me now several times a day, especially when we're talking about faulty sperm donors or my mother's illness.

"Everything happens for a reason, everything happens for a reason," over and over and over again.

At first the phrase comforts me, makes me feel like I'm in good hands. Then it starts to grate on me, feeling all too similar to "I don't want to talk about it" or "Stop complaining" or "Shut the fuck up."

By the time my sister is packing for her return to Los Angeles, I can't take it anymore.

"Things can just suck, you know, for no apparent reason. People get sick. People can't have babies. There are car accidents and diseases and war for no reason other than that's the way it goes. That's life on earth. Chaos. Arbitrary, random chaos. Life's not fair."

My sister pauses above her suitcase. "You are so negative," she tells me.

My sister's mantra, true or not, enables her to get on a plane and fly to California while her mother battles cancer 3,000 miles away. To that extent, it affords her peace of mind. Mine, on the other hand, leaves me a nervous dismal wreck. If the meaning of life is only what we tell ourselves, I really must get a new story.

In the days before my weekend shift at my mother's place, Faith and I make certain our new donor is available, that he hasn't been scooped up by all of the other artificially inseminating women in this great infertile country of ours. A general rule of thumb in the sperm-purchasing world is if a donor sounds good to you, then he sounds good to everyone else too. Working in our favor, however, is his mixed background. Not everyone, I imagine, is so willing to forsake their heritage just to grab the best-looking guy on the block.

My sister has come and gone. My uncle has come and gone. And even my brief stay is now over. Today is my mother's first day home alone. She's nestled again into the corner of her sectional sofa, reading the paper, talking on the phone, every so often gathering the strength to get up and go to the bathroom or into the kitchen to get something to eat or drink. She doesn't yet have the energy to clean up after herself should she find the energy to put food into a bowl. Someone has to come in three times a day to take the dog for a walk. I did everything I could think of before I left for work this morning: cleaned the tub for her evening bath, poured kibble into the dog's bowl so she wouldn't have to bend down. I prepared little one-step meals and labeled their containers. I call her every couple of hours from work, but there she is and here I am. Faith and I offered to take her into our home, to set her up in the spare room, but she refused.

On our way to the airport, my sister and I had a huge fight. I had made the apparent mistake of saying, "I wish I were going to L.A. tomorrow."

My sister blew from the soles of her feet to the blond half-highlighted hairs on her head. It was all about how I think her life is one big L.A. vacation—which I sometimes do—and that even when she's home away from winter and our mother's endless battle with cancer, she's still thinking about it *all* the time and, therefore, is forever tortured and never, ever free. I told her that she misunderstood me, that there are both positive and negative aspects to each of our positions, that I envy some things about her situation just as surely she must envy things about mine.

"There is nothing to envy about my position!" Her face is red with tears, rage. "Nothing!"

Two days after I return home from my mother's, my sister calls me from L.A., chipper, singsong. "I'm pregnant!" she says. "That's probably why I was feeling so emotional."

The Ides of March

(THE BLIZZARD THAT NEVER WAS AND MY MOTHER, MY SELF)

March is the suckiest of all months. The biggest, longest, baddest bitch of a month for anyone living in a snow zone. March is like gaining ten pounds or getting a really bad haircut. March is needing a root canal and a new timing belt for your car. March is cold and dark and long when you've already had four and a half months of cold and dark and long. March sucks. And then it's April. But first you have to get through March. To make matters worse, while our handsome new donor is in stock, his donation will not be out of quarantine until next month, so I'm ovulating a sad, lonely little egg without a chance in hell for fertilization, just a wasted, forgotten egg dropping down my fallopian tube for transport into the lining of an O.B. tampon. This time skipping a month feels like awful defeat, like suspended reproductive animation. And why this month? This egg? Sad little thing. No lights, no press, no fanfare. Ovulation without an audience. It's the closing of a Broadway show, Clinton after his presidency, a small town after its fifteen minutes of fame. Ovulation? Oh, am I ovulating? The egg goes off and becomes a drunk, clinging to the tampon with one hand, clutching a bottle of whiskey with the other. "I could've been someone." But nobody's listening. This cycle nobody even cares.

As if that weren't enough, we're awaiting the great blizzard of 2001. Weathermen and women threaten a storm larger than the one that dropped two feet of snow in 1978. They say this could be the largest storm ever to hit New England. I retrieve my mother and all of her groceries, a week's worth of medication and underwear, and transplant her in our house. She agrees because we are in for it, and if she doesn't come with me we may not see each other for weeks. That, and I've bought a box of her favorite doughnuts—toasted almond—fresh this morning from the shop up the road.

"Come with me and they're all yours..." It's enough to make even a die-hard independent like my mother throw her hands up in surrender.

A state of emergency is declared in advance. Nobody will be caught off-guard like in '78 when motorists were stranded for hours trying to get home from work. No, this time will be different. This time sophisticated meteorological technology will see to it that no man or woman has to abandon a car in a snowbank. It's all very exciting. Supermarkets have run out of milk and bread; neighbors who ordinarily ignore one another are chatting it up about snow shovels and ice melt and the state of their roofs. Regularly scheduled television is interrupted to broadcast the mayor of Boston, state troopers, and EMTs all serious and folksy in informal we-are-all-in-this-together wool sweaters and fleece hats. They advise all "nonessential" workers to stay home. Every school in the state is closed. Streets are cleared of cars. Snowplows line the curbs like tanks ready to roll at the first flake. Salters and sanders stand at attention. Medical emergency numbers loop over and over again on banners at the bottom of every television show.

It is 10 A.M. when the hospital declares our research department "nonessential" and I'm sent home to my mother and Faith and the kitty, to wait.

At 2 P.M. the snowless sky turns from gray to blue. What flurries there are turn to rain. The wind dies.

No one will admit the error. For hours newscasters go on trying to convince us we're still in for it, that this is just a lull, a calm before the storm. We wonder who will crack first, the mayor, the governor, or the weathermen and women.

Meanwhile, with everyone I love and wish to take care of under the same roof, I experience overwhelming relief. My stress and anxiety and vulnerability finally are contained to a manageable dull roar. For the time being there will be no shuttling to and from one concern to another. For the next twenty-four or thirty-six or seventy-two hours, however long it takes the city to release us, I'm free from having to choose between taking care of myself and taking care of my mother. Maybe it is harder for my sister after all, living so far away, having to choose her life over and over again.

For now we're at strange wintry peace, my mother in the bedroom on the telephone, Faith in the dining room working on her taxes. I should meditate, write, read, practice yoga. Instead I watch the sky. The wind returns. The cold gray. The rain freezes into snow. Maybe they are right after all.

Falling in Love

(*THE BRADY BUNCH* AND A VIAL OF GOOD SPERM)

Believe it or not, it was my sister who originally fixed Faith and me up. Faith and her sister had cast Carrie in a show they created, a stage production of *The Brady Bunch* titled *The Real Live Brady Bunch*. The original Jan had gone on to *Saturday Night Live,* and Carrie was selected to step in as Jan number two. After extended runs in Chicago, New York, and Los Angeles, the show was scheduled to go on a nationwide tour. First stop, Boston. At the opening night performance I followed my younger sister's instructions and went up to the musical director sitting at the piano: "My sister said I should say hello." The rest, as they say...

Faith and I spent the first year and a half of our relationship commuting across the country to see each other. She and a few other cast members had jumped ship when the tour landed in San Francisco, where they rented apartments and put up a new show called *Not Without My Nipples,* about a young girl who holds her family hostage until they consent to pay for her breast reduction. I had jumped my own ship—medical school. With a big fat one-year deferral in my pocket, I quit my job and moved in with Faith, first in San Francisco and then (after San Francisco gave *Not Without My Nipples* the finger) Los Angeles, where the show was a minor success. Because I could tolerate Los Angeles only in small, six-week doses, I wound up going back and forth, from L.A. to Boston, until my deferral ran out and I was forced to head home and face the medical music. Frustrated with the L.A. industry shuffle and curious about her ability to make it on her own as a musician, Faith joined me. Six years later, we periodically still question whether to return to Los Angeles, especially during the winter, or when a friend gets a job writing for television for like a million dollars a week, or when life here gets particularly heinous and stressful.

"Maybe we should have stayed in Los Angeles," I make the mistake of saying to Carrie on the phone one day during yet another conversation about how to best care for our mom.

"So move back!"

Everything happens for a reason!

So move back!

I haven't meditated for days and I feel great! I think meditation was depressing me, making me too calm. It's hard to exist in a chaotic world when you're on the verge of inner peace. So I throw in the towel. I watch an episode of the new *Survivor,* ruminate over the sounds coming from Margaret and Beth's apartment upstairs, over money and health and the state of my therapist's sex life (how often, what time of day, with whom).

Besides, who needs inner peace when hope has come to cast her golden rays across the horizon? It turns out the chemotherapy infusion has decimated the tumor in the left side of my mother's liver, there are two vials of "extraordinarily good-looking" sperm waiting for us next week, my agent sold a piece of my work, and it is warm enough today to go outside without a coat!

At night I even dream of an article in the Sunday paper, a series of interviews with children and their parents. There are pictures of smiling, energetic children of gay parents and quiet, unassuming children of heterosexual parents. The children of the heterosexuals, the reader soon learns, are all developmentally delayed, challenged, retarded. While the children of gay parents are healthy, sane, robust.

An otherwise sane lesbian we know who just had a baby has gone crazy! The story about town is that she cannot stand breast-feeding. She wants to stop cold turkey and sleep at a friend's house overnight while her partner gets up every two hours to give the baby formula in a bottle. The biological mom had wanted a baby for *years*. It was her partner who had to be convinced it was worth laying down her autonomy, her desire to work twelve-hour days and worry over nothing but stray dogs, in order to raise real live human children.

"She's not making sense," the partner says of bio-mom.

But bio-mom has it all planned out: She will live down the block with Tory, there will be no more breast-feeding, no more sleepless nights, her partner will raise the baby. Last I heard, they were going to consult with a psychologist.

Clutching the promise of our new batch of super-duper sperm, Faith and I fire the awful private for-profit fertility clinic and Dr. $ and have the precious juice shipped directly to the really nice hospital-based fertility clinic recommended by my new, really nice obstetrician. There, the plan is to perform blood tests and ultrasounds to determine exactly when it is that I'm ovulating. On the telephone, the new fertility clinic is even nicer than I remember. They are proactive, conservative, gay-friendly, and really, really, nice.

At my mother's, the night before her second chemoembolization and a week or so before the first insemination of the rest of our lives, I try to lighten the mood with a little racist humor. "If I don't get pregnant with this new donor," I announce, "maybe I'll switch to an African-American one."

"Oy," my mother responds. "Don't you think you're going to have enough aggravation?"

"Uh-oh," says Faith.

At times of crisis the truth slips out. My mother still has reservations about two women raising a child. But how can you be mad at someone who is facing a dangerous medical procedure that may or may not save her life? I think I just feel bad. It rhymes with mad, but is lower on the scale of cognitive unrest. I feel bad and sad, but not mad. After everything that has happened and is about to happen, after Faith and I have moved into her home for five days to help her heal, my mother is still disappointed in our lifestyle, still feels her daughter is not living to her potential and will be bringing a child into a world of, if not hardship and scrutiny, then at the very least, aggravation. On the brink of another cancer-related challenge, I don't have my mother's blessing or her optimism. I still haven't made the grade. If this were any other moment in our life together, I would ask her to explain what she means, engage her in a lengthy emotional debate. But it's the night before part two of a dangerous procedure we pray will save her life, so I let it go, chalk it up to the outdated script she cannot let go of in her head.

"Your mother thinks you're mad at her," Faith tells me as we get ready for a long, nervous night on a pull-out couch in my mother's guest room.

I give my mother a kiss good night and in the morning hold her hand as we wait for hours at the hospital.

That night in my dreams my therapist yells at me, "Get out of here!" And then Faith announces she will be sleeping, once a week, with the man who is scheduled to tile our kitchen. In my dreams I'm abandoned by the two other women of importance in my life.

The crazy lesbian mom is no longer crazy, no longer rambling incoherently about switching her infant daughter to formula and sleeping away from home. Apparently, she stopped one of her night feedings, got more rest, and is normal again. It turned out she wasn't crazy—just really, really tired.

This time there is no visit to the emergency room, no heart rate of 180 or fever of 103. There is just my mother in her nest in the corner of the sofa unable to do much more than eat, drink, and make jokes. We are grateful. We are grateful for some many things: the return of spring, the Arnold Arboretum, the daffodils and cherry trees, the lush purple and pink rhododendrons. We are grateful for the hope of this procedure, for the fact that we only live ten minutes away and have lives flexible enough to enable us to care for my mother.

We are grateful for new sperm, for the fact that my pregnant sister is coming in two days to relieve us.

In between visits to my mother, I race off for blood work and ultrasounds. The first ultrasound takes place on day nine of my cycle and reveals not a follicle in sight. Apparently, both ovaries are "suppressed" and empty. The technician tells me this as if I will become despondent at the news of my shrunken vacant ovaries, but I'm overjoyed.

"So there are no cysts or tumors?"

"Oh, no. They're really very suppressed, quite small."

Hallelujah! I know this may not be the best news with regard to the current state of my fertility, but as far as ovarian cancer goes, I'm in the clear. I explain this all to the technician so she can make sense of my relief.

"I see," she says—though I don't think she does—and instructs me to return three days later for another ultrasound.

"Isn't three days a long time? What if I ovulate between now and then?"

"From the size of your ovaries and the fact that there are no follicles, I'd say that's highly unlikely."

She was wrong. We missed this month's egg. The little sucker blew in and out of town too fast, like she was just here for a quick meeting. Well, who needs her anyway, the frenzied type-A egg. It's back to the drawing board, but who cares.

Even though the first seven months of this trying-to-get pregnant business supposedly shouldn't count, even though we're really just now beginning, it still feels like it's been forever. I still feel worn out and depleted, tired of fitting my feet into stirrups every month, tired of living in fear of my period, tired of calculating ovulation like a chemist attempting to predict the exact moment a compound will turn from liquid to gas. I can't even remember sometimes what we're trying to achieve. A baby? All of this medicine, and technology, and money, and timing has to do with having a baby?

Margaret has taken to spending long hours in the back-yard holding Phoebe up to the sky. They giggle and gurgle and glow. I'm convinced she's out to get me, that her joy is calculated, conspiratorial. Why they would want to hurt me like this I have no idea. In response I have taken to referring to Margaret and Beth as "the lesbians," as in "Will the les-bians *ever* take the garbage out?" I'm sure this has inter-nalized homophobia written all over it, but I don't care. I am under siege.

Faith rolls her eyes. "Not everything has to do with you."

If only that were true.

Winter Into Spring

I dream I'm trying to unlock the door to my car and get inside—should that be so difficult? But there are children in the parking lot or on the street where I am trying to accomplish this—little boys—and they are running wild and out of control, getting in my way as I try to get into my car.

"Move your monkeys!" I shout at their mother, who is looking on. "Keep your monkeys under control!"

One of the little boys looks at me jeeringly. "Monkeys are always girls, and I'm a boy, so I can't be a monkey."

"Of course monkeys can be boys, you little fuck," I say.

"Mommy, that woman said 'fuck.' "

I turn to the entire family now gathered round and gaping at me and yell, "Fuck! Fuck! Fuck! Fuck! Fuck!"

And then the weather changes. It's been a long, slow crawl, but spring is finally here. Each year it seems entirely possible that winter will never ever leave, and why should it? It only has to return four months later. Why even bother to pack its bags and head south of the equator. But then a crocus pops its yellow or blue or purple or pink head up from the earth, to signal the daffodils that the coast is clear. The daffies alert the forsythia and they send up a golden "GO!" to the magnolias and the dogwoods and soon there are leaves on the trees and it's hard to remember why there's a shovel and a bag of ice-melt on your porch.

Faith and I walk whenever we can. We spend a weekend in Manhattan wandering around the lower east side and Chinatown, in and out of department stores on Broadway. We crisscross the working-class blocks of our neighborhood, tour around the Victorian-lined streets near my mother's town house. We walk up and down hills at the arboretum, weaving our way around cherry trees and white spruce, hemlock trees and black walnut.

There are a hundred million dogs in the arboretum, each being led by a lesbian couple and their child. It's true. For every flowering blossom there is a lesbian, and for every lesbian there is a baby. It's overwhelming, mind-boggling, an epidemic. If one were only to frequent parks like the Arnold Arboretum one might surmise that all American families consisted of two moms in jeans, a baby in overalls, and a Labrador-shepherd mix. Just as there are among heterosexual families, there are kind-looking lesbian families, the harried and overworked, the gentle and relaxed, and the cold and aloof. We are just another couple among many. Our children, should we ever have them, will be just more kids among kids. So long as we don't venture too far from the Arnold Arboretum, all will be well. We will be mainstream, just like the scenery.

$\mathcal{KD}$3?

(Two Steps Forward, One Step Back)

We are smooth sailing. My mother is living on her own after only two and a half weeks. She still needs help with meals and laundry and walking the dog, but today she made her bed and was able to go up her flight of fifteen stairs twice. Twice! We're even counting down again to the next round of ultrasounds and the first insemination of the rest of our lives. It's down to the single digits, four days until ultrasound number one. They've called out the reserves this time. There will be an ultrasound and then daily blood tests. The goal is to time to the nearest twelve-hour period the momentous moment of my ovulation and then to inject me with two rounds of fertile, mixed-race sperm.

But then, in the final hour, Eric, the guitarist who stayed too long, comes back from Spain. He is in town for two weeks to play a special encore performance of Faith's rock opera. It's a bit of déjà vu: ovulation–rock opera–Eric week. He's decided not to stay with us this time, and that